Ninjas,

Piranhas,

and

Galileo

Ninjas,

Piranhas,

and

Galileo

BY GREG LEITICH SMITH

LITTLE, BROWN AND COMPANY
New York ✌ An AOL Time Warner Company

First Edition

The characters and events portrayed in this book are fictitious. Any similarity to real persons, living or dead, is coincidental and not intended by the author.

Library of Congress Cataloging-in-Publication Data

Smith, Greg Leitich.
Ninjas, piranhas, and Galileo / Greg Leitich Smith—1st ed.
p. cm.
Summary: Honoria, Shohei, and Elias, who are "united together against That Which Is The Peshtigo School," face conflict over their budding romantic interest and a science project gone awry.
ISBN 0-316-77854-0
[1. Science projects — Fiction. 2. Schools — Fiction. 3. Japanese Americans — Fiction.
4. Family life — Illinois — Chicago — Fiction. 5. Chicago (Ill.) — Fiction.] I. Title.

PZ7.S6488Ni 2003
[Fic] — dc21   2003047629

10 9 8 7 6 5 4 3 2 1

Q-FF

Printed in the United States of America

The text for this book was set in Criterion Light, and the display type is Eaglefeather.

For Cyn

Ninjas,

Piranhas,

and

Galileo

Chapter 1

Can You Teach a Piranha to Eat a Banana?

Elias

I knew I was in trouble when I heard the cello.

Bach. The Suite for Unaccompanied Cello No. 6, in D Major, BWV 1012.

In my family, you learn music young and you learn it classical. I was five before I realized there was any other kind. I was seven before I figured out not everybody thought country music was "a gross and diabolical assault on the senses."

Anyway, Dad almost never practices the Suites unless he's working on a grant proposal, trying to avoid editing a paper for the *American Journal of Articles About Physics that No One Can Understand,* or unless he just wants to torture our purebred weimaraner, Beastmaster VII.

At the time, I was sprawled across my bed, supposedly

doing algebra homework. I may only be in the seventh grade, but at the Peshtigo School of Chicago, they believe in "All Math, All the Time." That's why I was on the phone, going over problems (well, answers) with my friend Shohei. He'd called twenty minutes earlier ("Quick, Elias, what's the answer to number seven?").

We'd been friends since halfway through second grade when Shohei transferred in from Palo Alto. He'd marched in, took the seat next to me, and introduced himself: "Hi, my name's Shohei." Then he'd reached into his backpack. "This is Mathilda."

It was his pet boa constrictor.

A couple of minutes later, Shohei introduced himself to the principal.

Now, we were on speakerphone, discussing how old Billy was if two years ago he was twice the square of his sister's age, when I heard Dad's cello playing through the air ducts. Beastmaster VII sat up, baying in counterpoint.

"You're in trouble now," Shohei said. He knew the signs, too.

I hung up the phone and ran upstairs. My dad was in his third-floor tower den, attacking his cello with the bow, looking like he was trying to slice its strings in two.

When I knocked on the door frame and walked in, Dad pointed at me, his bow's tip touching my chest.

"You," he announced, "will be participating in your school science fair this year."

Dad pulled a sheet of paper off his music stand and thrust it at me. "That school of yours," he added, "to which I pay more in tuition than my undergraduates pay at the University of Chicago, once again has asked me to be the chief judge."

"Everyone else's parents are lawyers," I said. Not quite, but my dad, Dr. Erich Brandenburg, was, in fact, the only parent of a Peshtigo Warrior Penguin with a Ph.D. in physics. And, music, of course. But I didn't think the Science Fair Committee would have been interested in that. I made the obvious connection: "You're going to use me to get out of it."

"Smart boy," Dad replied, smiling with just his teeth. "Couldn't be too fair, could I, with my own son participating?"

I knew better than to say anything further when Dad was being decisive. He returned to his Bach, and Beastmaster VII began howling again. Dismissed, I dragged the dog with me back downstairs.

The thing was, I didn't do science fairs. Ever. And Dad knew it. My oldest brother (of four), Johann Christoph — the one who'd finally finished his Ph.D. dissertation and had just started his postdoc at Cambridge University — had been the one who always did math and science for fun and profit.

And my only sister, Anna. But she had left for West Point last summer, and her twin, Johann Jakob, was off to the University of Texas, leaving me the only one still at home. As for my other brothers, Johann Michael's been busy doing whatever he does at college in Hawaii, and no one's seen Johann Ambrosius since he went to work for the government. So, with Mom gone until Christmas on a concert tour of Australia, there was nothing to stop Dad from being all . . . Dad.

I walked back into my room as the phone rang. Shohei, I figured, trying to scam the solution to the extra-credit problem. Instead, it was Honoria, my best friend who happens to be a girl. As opposed to my girlfriend.

At least that's what I told people.

"Two questions, Eli," she said. "Number one: Can you teach a piranha to eat a banana? Number two: Do you think Shohei would go out with me?"

The Peshtigo School of Chicago has a reputation for being highly intense. We have to take at least one foreign language, all kinds of math and science, a musical instrument, a fall or spring sport, and at least one nonathletic extracurricular activity.

The Gloriana Biddulph Memorial Science Fair Gold Medal is considered one of the Peshtigo School's "prestige" awards. It's also extremely geeky, and it's very weird that so many people take it seriously, but then, you could say the same about the Super Bowl. What all that means, though, is that if you do a project for the science fair, you have to do something spectacular. Worse, it counts extra toward your science grade, even though it's almost impossible to get an A, and has even been known to bring your grade down.

Don't get me wrong. Honoria and I are considered two of the Smart Ones. It's expected.

That's why I spent five unsuccessful hours Saturday afternoon trying to come up with a sufficiently grand project of my own. I even considered calling Honoria to see if she had a suggestion. She always does a project for the science fair, and she's been out to win the gold medal for years.

But after some thought, I decided that calling her wouldn't be such a good idea. Honoria can get very competitive. So I didn't think she'd be too happy to just hand over, free of charge, an entire project. Besides, her science fair projects can be unusual, even by the standards of the Peshtigo School.

Sunday morning, I finally had an inspiration. As soon as Dad and I got home from church, I headed down to the Brandenburg Archives. They're located in our finished basement, and are the repository of everything Brandenburg. They're made up of about twenty, four-drawer legal-sized file cabinets housing report cards; homework, exam, and dissertation files; birth certificates and pedigree papers; fingerprints; the opera Dad wrote; a collection of post-op wisdom teeth; and, most importantly, each and every science project ever committed by a Brandenburg.

I started with Christoph's and Anna's files of school science projects. I wasn't (just) trying to find an easy way out. My idea came from one of the prime commandments of modern science: *Thou shalt obtain experimental confirmation.* Like how Galileo is supposed to have dropped cannonballs of different weights off the Leaning Tower of Pisa to see if he could prove Aristotle's theory that they would hit the ground at different times.

I figured I could play Galileo to Christoph's or Anna's Aristotle and redo one of their projects to see if I could confirm their results.

I scanned a few of the subjects: "Is Coca-Cola a corrosive?" "Do duck quacks echo?" "Will a three-headed planaria learn to navigate a maze more quickly than a single-headed one?" (Note: They're not *born* with three heads.)

I pulled the experiment that looked easiest.

Chapter 2

Plants, Music, and ∫ushi

Honoria

I became friends with Eli because of the naked mole rat, *Heterocephalus glaber,* a small, wrinkled, communal, and oddly insectlike rodent, and because the Peshtigo School offers its kindergartners the chance to spend a night, with "appropriate adult supervision," at the Lincoln Park Zoo.

Even though Eli and I had both enrolled for kindergarten the same year, we didn't actually meet until the zoo outing that November because Eli was in the morning session and I went in the afternoon.

As was usual, there was some yelling and screaming about which of the animal pavilions we were to see before dark. A majority of my classmates wanted to see the chimpanzees at the Great Ape House. When I said that I preferred to go to the Small Mammal and Reptile House, because small mammals and reptiles were less creepy than great apes, the only person who agreed with me or, perhaps more accurately, didn't mock me, was this kid in black plastic-framed glasses, whose mother, a large woman with a large voice, was one of the chaperones.

While I wouldn't have minded going alone, I remember being grateful someone wanted to come with me. Later that night, though, after we'd had our fill of naked mole rats, Eli's mother embarrassed us both by brushing his brown bangs out of his eyes and telling him, in front of everyone, that he had been "the perfect little gentleman."

At the moment, he was being less than perfect, though he didn't have that bangs problem anymore. We were in the hall between classes in front of my locker, and Eli was telling me that he intended to copy his brother Christoph's old experiment on whether music affects plant growth.

"How is it not cheating?" I asked Eli, locking directly onto his blue-gray eyes. His newest oval wire-framed glasses were a significant improvement.

He didn't blink. But he didn't answer right away, either. A second later, I handed Eli a pair of double-sided glue pads that I was going to use for attaching an ant farm to my locker door. It would replace my tattered poster, ARACHNIDS OF NORTH AMERICA.

"It's *valid*," Eli replied, finally. "Like Galileo and the Leaning Tower. Third party experimental confirmation —"

"True enough," I said, fixing the glue pads in place on the back of the ant farm. "I can quote *Intro to History of Science*, too. But the fact of the matter is, you don't really want to confirm Christoph's results, you want to do as little work as possible. Including, I might add, having to come up with an idea of your own."

"So?" Eli said, leaning against the edge of my locker door. "You're the one who likes the science fair. I'm only doing it because my dad's making me. Besides, the science fair judges don't score for originality."

That much was true. Christopher Robin Reed — "Goliath Reed" to both friends and enemies — had won the science fair three years running with really stupid consumer-product related experiments and somewhat awesome multimedia presentations. Last year, his project was about which brand of paper towel was the most absorbent. The specific gravity calculations were impressive, but still.

"Well," I replied, sticking the ant farm in place, "what do you think Mr. Eden will say?"

Mr. Ethan Eden was a science teacher and the sponsor of the science fair. He had been teaching at the Peshtigo School long enough to have outlasted three deans of the elementary school, six mayors of Chicago, and seven presidents of the

United States. And he had taught every one of Eli's brothers and sisters. He's not a bad teacher, just dull, humorless, bitter, and sometimes mean.

"Already taken care of," Eli said, crossing his arms, looking a little too smug.

I raised an eyebrow. "He approved it?" I asked.

Eli nodded, then asked, not subtly, "What do you think Goliath Reed is going to do his project on this year?"

"I don't care," I said, letting Eli change the subject. "He's not going to win." I smiled. "And neither are you."

Shohei

It was lunch, it was Friday, and Elias and I were sitting at our usual table in the school cafeteria. That meant that I was trading the sushi my mom had made for Elias's roast beef sandwich.

Since the beginning of the school year, my mom had been getting up two and a half hours early every day to make and roll a fresh batch. This probably wouldn't be all that unusual if we were living in, say, Nagasaki, and our name was Morimoto. But we live in Chicago, and our name is O'Leary. As in the cow and the fire.

See, I'm adopted and am actually Japanese American.

My parents are Irish American. It's why my name is Shohei O'Leary and why my parents have started doing things like preparing the food of the Land of the Shogun every day of the week.

Seaweed, fish, and rice.

Don't get me wrong: I like sushi sometimes — and my mom's has gotten much better — but occasionally, like any red-blooded American, crave something cooked, like a hot dog. Or baby-back ribs.

Being a Chicagoan, I'd worked out a system. A couple times a week, I'd trade the sushi for whatever Honoria or Elias brought from home, or for a trip through the award-winning Peshtigo School cafeteria line. It usually isn't as bad as Elias makes it out to be. Sure, the place smells a bit like ammonia, the stuff's a little greasy, and the hamburgers are mostly soy, but at least the Jell-O isn't too soupy, and there's always the Tater Tots.

"What's today's choice?" Elias asked, peering into the Tupperware container.

"Guess," I said, through a mouthful of roast beef and sourdough.

"*Tekka, kappa, futomaki,*" Elias pointed with his chop-sticks, glancing at me to see if he'd gotten it right.

I swallowed, then nodded, deciding not to correct his pro-nunciation.

"But what's this?" He held up the roll of nori filled with a clump of what looked like brown paste.

"That's the special," I said. He turned it over, stared at it like he was scared it would bite, and sniffed.

"*Uni,*" I told him.

He put it in his mouth, then made a face.

"Sea urchin," I translated.

He spit it out, then quickly wiped his tongue with a napkin.

"It's a delicacy," I said, which was what my mom had told me.

Honoria

Back when Eli introduced me to Shohei the first time, I complimented his English.

"That's very nice of you," he replied after a moment. "Yours is good, too. You've got kind of a funny accent, though."

To this day, he claims I have a Chicago accent.

Yes, I felt less than intelligent. But Frederika Murchison-Kowalski had told me that the new transfer student was Japanese and that he was the son of someone from the

consulate and that's why he'd brought a boa constrictor —
Lichanura trivirgata — to school. It made more sense at the
time.

From then on, though, Shohei, Eli, and I had been sort of
a gang of three, united together against That Which Is the
Peshtigo School. I didn't want to be the one responsible for
breaking it up, which is what I was afraid would happen if I
told Shohei I thought he looked like Keanu Reeves, but less
vapid, and all he said in response was "That's very nice of
you."

We would still probably be friends, but there would always be that awkwardness that comes from deep and eternal
humiliation, which was why I was hoping that Eli would find
out for me if Shohei was interested, but Eli became a little
disturbed when I brought it up the other night. So I decided
I had to get Shohei to notice me on my own. Or his.

Chapter 3

Planning Ahead

Shohei

It was after soccer practice, and Elias and I were at a window booth at Eisenberg's, a diner and ice cream joint across the street from the Peshtigo School. It's a great place, if you can get over the fact that every other song has words like "boogedy" and "shoop" in it. It's got a lot of chrome and neon and mirrors and is supposed to be an "authentic" 1950s-style diner. It even has the front and rear ends of a '57 Chevy sticking out of different walls. The banana splits and cheese fries are killer, though.

We were talking about Honoria. Aside from being a Smart One, she's not bad to look at. Shoulder-length brown hair, eyes almost the same shade, in decent shape from the swim team. Her nose is a little big, though.

"I'm telling you, she likes you," I said, gesturing with a fry. Elias had been mooning over her since last year's science fair. By now, I was ready to have him do something or shut up about it. Besides, I didn't see what the big deal was. The two of them spent a ton of time together already.

"Honoria does not like me," he replied, sipping his vanilla milk shake.

I dipped the cheddar fry in my banana split juice and ate it before replying. "She calls you 'Eli.'"

He shrugged. "She's known me a long time."

"I've known you almost as long, and I don't call you 'Eli.'"

Elias inspected his glasses, then wiped one lens. "Because I'd beat you if you did."

I leaned back against the window and stretched my legs onto the vinyl bench. "You like her; she likes you. What's the problem?" Of course, so far as I knew, neither Elias nor Honoria had ever even held hands with a member of the opposite sex. I, on the other hand, once kissed Freddie M-K, or at least tried, but she ended up with spit in her eye. I got that Elias was worried about making a fool of himself, but he seemed more worried about it than usual. Maybe he was just totally scared she'd say "no," or laugh at him or something, but that's not her style.

Elias looked like he was about to say something, but before he got the chance, I heard a car horn and glanced out the window. My mom had pulled up in our new electric-blue VW Beetle. As we dumped some money onto the table to pay for the food, I asked Elias, "If I can prove to you that she likes you, will you ask her out?"

He gave me a weird look. "If you can find out . . . anonymously," he said.

"Deal," I replied as we headed to the car.

Honoria
The Peshtigo Warrior Penguin battle cry and war dance were designed by a famous and well-paid choreographer to strike terror into the hearts of opposing teams. They're actually more like a waddle, head bob, and groan, and just look silly. They're even more ridiculous when Goliath Reed performs them in the Student Court courtroom after a verdict in his favor.

The Student Court is the Peshtigo School's pride, joy, and number-one propaganda tool. It's mentioned in all our publicity literature, and it was even featured in *Newsweek* magazine. Apparently, at some schools, the Student Court only decides punishment, after the accused admits guilt. At the Peshtigo School, the accused is innocent until proven guilty. We'd originally had it the other way, but a whole horde of lawyers from the Parent-Teacher Senate protested.

I was the Public Defender, which meant I was chief defense attorney. I had been defending Freddie Murchison-Kowalski, the head of the Union of Students Concerned About Cruelty to Animals, who had put together and posted on bulletin boards around the school a list of "101 Ways to Kill a Person with a Chicken-Fried Steak." She said it was a protest against inhumane treatment of cattle, hormones in beef, cholesterol, and the school cafeteria.

Freddie was on trial for "malicious hooliganism," which is a catchall for anything the administration doesn't like or thinks would make the school look bad to generous alums or to *Newsweek* magazine. Goliath Reed was serving a term as Attorney General, which made him the chief prosecutor, and had been arguing that Freddie's protest posed a threat to the public safety and could even lead to violence.

Incredibly, the jury bought it.

When the guilty verdict was announced, Freddie sat there, looking stunned, because I'd told her we'd win. Meanwhile, Goliath jumped up, pumped his fist, and yelled, "Yes!" After that, he and his assistant did their ferocious Penguin display.

After they high-fived, Goliath smirked, flashing me four fingers.

Four cases in a row, he meant, that he'd beaten me.

I don't mind losing. I just don't like losing to Goliath Reed.

Elias

Last year, my only sister, Anna, scored big at nationals with her science project involving three-headed planaria. We had a big family celebration down at Anna and Johann Jakob's favorite Bavarian restaurant, Do Your Wurst. Of course, by then, "big family celebration" meant only Mom, Dad, Anna, Jake, and me. The rest hadn't been able to fly in for the weekend.

It was last year during Anna's planaria project that I realized I thought of Honoria as more than a friend. Right after Honoria found out what Anna's project was, she'd started bombarding me with e-mails: How long can you make the cuts before you kill the worm, or get three, instead of one with three heads? How sharp a razor blade do you need? What happens if you make a partial sideways or full cut? What happens if you cauterize the cut while you're making it?

Until Honoria's e-mails, Anna's project had just been this big inconvenience occupying the dining room table with slimy vermin. But Honoria was so eager, so excited, it was hard not to get at least a little interested. Like some warped spectator sport. I was intrigued, and not just by the planaria.

Chapter 4

The Garden

Honoria

The Atrium Garden at the Peshtigo School is, in my humble opinion, the school's most impressive architectural feature and, according to the plaque on the outside, the Fellows of the American Architectural Institute agree. The Garden is most popular after lunch; the administration only allows in twenty-five students on any one day, and only if they have the lucky lottery number, although Shohei tells me there's a black market for winning tickets.

The Garden has zones maintained at constant temperature and humidity for Mr. Eden's collection of tropical plants. Each one is labeled with its English and scientific names and classical chamber music always plays from hidden speakers.

In fact, it had been Christoph Brandenburg's science project — the one Eli was copying — that had convinced Mr. Eden to start with the chamber music and to ban anything else.

As usual, Eli and I went around left — it's less crowded — to find an open bench. We finally found one on the far side opposite the wrought-iron gate, near the koi pond, with a view of the hurricane and cabbage palms and an assortment of ferns.

We'd just settled down on the bench when I looked up to see Shohei running toward us — arms wide, wearing his usual Chicago Cubs baseball cap — across the edge of the Memorial Fountain of the Grand Army of the Republic.

"Do you love me?" Shohei shouted.

I had a mild panic attack as what Shohei said sunk in and yanked my headphones down to rest around my neck. "Eli, you promised not to tell him I told you I liked him."

"I didn't," Eli whispered back. "He's just being Shohei."

On the last syllable, Shohei himself landed in front of us and repeated, "Do you love me?" His eyes were wide, he was smiling, and he clearly wanted something.

"That depends," Eli said.

"Ple-e-e-ease," Shohei begged, turning it into a four-syllable word as he fell to his knees beside the bench, trampled a coromandel plant, and clutched at my skirt. "Help me, help me, help me."

I glanced around. Nobody was paying attention. Every-one was used to him.

I could guess what he wanted. Shohei's parents always made him do a science project, the deadline for the science fair was tomorrow, and Shohei always waited as long as possible to decide anything. Last year, I had, in fact, gone insane and agreed at the last minute to let him team up with me on my project. His efforts were, to put it mildly, horrible, and during the judging he seared his eyebrows with my Bunsen burner.

It was not going to happen this year. He may be, as they say, a hottie, but I'm not stupid.

Sure enough, Shohei announced, "I need a science proj-ect of my very own. Or" — he smiled — "one of yours."

Before I could say "no," firmly and politely, Mr. Eden, the science fair czar, swooped out of nowhere and demanded, "What. Is. That. Noise?"

Shohei scrambled up out of the way to stand back on the path.

Mr. Eden seized my headphones from around my neck. I turned the volume all the way down and psyched myself for whatever he was going to do.

"Well?" Mr. Eden demanded, glaring down.

"Nat King Cole," I replied, hoping the CD was on the "ap-proved" list and kicking myself for not checking recently.

Mr. Eden shuddered. "You know the rules," he replied, pulling a handkerchief from his vest pocket and using it to remove the CD from my Discman. "No non-approved music in the Atrium Garden."

"That's my mother's," I protested, as Mr. Eden's attention shifted to Josh Patel, who was trying to hide a contraband bottle of root beer behind an Abyssinian banana tree. Food and drink were, of course, forbidden.

"You may have it back after school," Mr. Eden said, still clutching the CD with the handkerchief as he stalked off toward Josh.

As soon as Mr. Eden was safely out of the way, Shohei sat back down in front of us and returned to begging Eli and me. "Can you help me out here, folks?" he asked, crossing his legs. "Anyone need an assistant?"

"Sorry," I said quickly, "piranhas don't like strangers. Eli might need a control, though." It may not have been altogether fair and siccing Shohei's unhelpfulness on Eli wasn't necessarily a nice thing to do, but it would help Shohei and it might make Eli do some actual work and how fair was it, anyway, that Eli was just copying his brother's project? I was still amazed that Mr. Eden had approved it. I wouldn't have.

Shohei got up on his knees, clasping his hands under his chin. I ignored his puppy-dog eyes, but I did nudge Eli. There were a couple moments of silence, or actually, baroque flute music, while Shohei looked at us expectantly. Then there were a couple more.

"I'm running Christoph's plant-music experiment," Eli said, finally. "Maybe you could do it at your place too, so we could . . . I don't know . . . see if there's a difference in growth conditions between Ravenswood Manor and Lincoln Park."

Shohei lives only about thirty minutes from Castle Brandenburg, and that's during rush hour, if you drive. "A difference from what?" he asked. "The tides?"

"Look, do you want to do it or not?" Eli asked.

"Okay, okay," Shohei said, adjusting his cap. "Just one more thing," he added, "anyone want to go see *Kabuki Titus Andronicus* this Saturday?"

We had just read *Titus Andronicus* in class, because our English teacher wanted us to know that Shakespeare had written some bad plays, too. But Mr. Garcia gave me extra readings on literary criticism when I told him I liked it better than *Hamlet* because Tamora — apart from the murder, vengeance, cannibalism, and blood pies — was a better role model than Ophelia, who drowned herself because of a man.

Eli shook his head. "I'm going to see *Der Rosenkavalier* at the Lyric with my dad."

"Uh-huh," Shohei replied, giving Eli a look. Then he turned to me. "How about you?"

"Love to," I told Shohei, jumping at the chance. Since

I didn't see Shohei much outside of school without Eli, it sounded like the perfect chance to get to him socially, alone, and maybe then he'd notice me in a more romantic way.

"Great," he replied.

"It'll just be us, then," I said to Shohei, the words just sort of slipping out. What I said was fine, but my tone was a little gushy. This, I hoped he wouldn't notice.

"Well," Shohei said, "us and my parents, anyway."

Shohei

I cornered Elias after lunch on the way to algebra.

"The opera?" I asked. "The opera? How dense are you? I just gave you the perfect chance to be alone with Honoria . . ."

"We have a box every season," Elias replied. "You know that."

Yeah, opera was big in their family. Elias's mom's a famous soprano. Travels around the world. Sings a lot. Blah, blah, blah.

"Get out of it," I said.

"Can't," Elias replied. He was quiet for a moment as we dodged hallway crowds. "And," he continued, in his annoyed tone of voice, as we reached the classroom, "since when does 'alone' include your parents and kid brother? Besides, I already spend a lot of time alone with Honoria."

"First," I replied in the same tone, "I was going to get my dad to get separate seats for you guys and, second, studying together and going to the Field Museum of Natural History to see dead bugs and stuffed ancient Egyptians does not count."

Man, this was going to be harder than I'd thought.

Chapter 5

Tatami Ninjas

Shohei

Monday afternoon after soccer practice, Elias and I came back to my place to get my part of the project set up. We live in a twenty-ninth-floor rooftop condo on Lake Shore Drive in Lincoln Park, with a clear view of the zoo and the lake. It rules.

"So, Honoria definitely likes you," I told Elias as we left our Nikes at the door. "She talked about you all night."

He just grunted, hoisting a box of project supplies.

"How was the opera?" I asked.

"Fine," he replied. "Why don't we get the project set up?"

If he wasn't ready to talk about Honoria yet, that was okay by me.

I led the way, carrying boxes to the guest bedroom.

"How's this?" I asked, setting down a box. I pulled open the drapes to the floor-to-ceiling, wall-to-wall windows overlooking the rush-hour traffic on Lake Shore Drive. The lake was choppy and empty. Most people had already put their sailboats in winter storage.

"No," Elias said. "We need a different room. The light's bad."

"Bad?" I asked. "What does that mean?"

"*Brassica rapa* is designed to grow in fluorescent light," Elias said. "It's easier to control that way. Didn't you read the draft of experimental procedures I e-mailed you yesterday?"

To be honest, I had just sort of skimmed it. But it still sounded nutty — how can light be bad for a plant? Other than, say, a death-ray laser, or something. But it was his project, so I figured I'd just go with it.

"It's specially developed for classroom use," Elias continued. "Don't you have a work or storage room downstairs or something?"

"Storeroom's full," I said, sitting down on the guest bed. "Your cheesehead cabbages will just have to be happy here."

"Wisconsin Fast Plants," he said. "And they're a member of the crucifer family."

"Whatever," I answered, but I was beginning to think maybe I should have come up with my own project. Whenever Elias gets into something, he gets pretty uptight about it.

"Well," he said, "I guess we can tape over the windows

and just unplug your lamps." He opened the boxes and began to pull out stuff. Seeds. Dirt. Fluorescent tubes. Watering can. Pots. Soundproofed light boxes. CD players. Noise meter. CD called *The Best of Baroque.* CD of water rushing over Niagara Falls. CD called *Her Britannic Majesty's Royal Gurkha Drum and Bagpipe Corps.* Then Elias began to explain. Everything. "Here's all you have to do . . ."

Just before my brains oozed out my nose from boredom, I got him to stop by humming *Scotland the Brave* and trying to balance the plastic watering can — by the spout — on my index finger. I mean, it's not like I couldn't figure this all out myself.

"Look," Elias said, finally, holding up a diskette. "This is the final draft of the project procedures. It's practically *Horticulture for the Intellectually Challenged.* Let me print it out for you."

Ignoring the slam, I led the way across the hall to my bedroom so he could use my computer.

"Wow," Elias said from behind.

I'd forgotten — he hadn't seen it yet. I turned around and spread my arms. "Welcome," I said, "to the Land of the Rising Sun." My room had been redone as part of my folks' Japanization effort. I did have an east view — toward the rising sun. The remodel was better than the last version of my room, but I was beginning to think my parents were out of control.

Until a few weeks ago, I'd had a great big, queen-sized, hideously ugly canopied bed my mom had bought when she'd been in her French Second Empire phase (it looks just like it sounds). I also used to have a matching Napoleon III desk and shelves as well as a red-and-gold carpet with a lot of flowers and stuff that defied description.

Now, a bunch of three-foot-by-three-foot *tatami* mats covered the floor and one wall had a wood-framed grid of rice paper. My bed had been replaced with this *tatami* thing that looked kind of like a coffee table, and the rest of the furniture was sort of short and came from Olaf of the Orient: A Fusion of West and East. Oh, and my framed and autographed World Cup soccer and Chicago Cubs posters had been replaced by a bamboo scroll and a silk print of a big wave with Mount Fuji in the background.

While Elias gazed around at the Japaneseness of it all, my five-year-old kid brother Tim sat cross-legged in the legless *zaisu* floor chair thing in front of the laptop computer. The laptop rested on the new, two-foot tall desk, next to Mathilda's tank.

Tim ignored us, typing away. Every now and then, he'd shrug to adjust his black cape. Tim is the kid my parents weren't supposed to be able to have. He's got light brown hair, freckles, green eyes, is missing his two front teeth, and his skin burns like crazy in the summer. Actually, he looks a little like Elias.

"I sort of like it," Elias said, "but why?"

"Here," I replied, rummaging through a pile of books on one of the shelves. I handed Elias last spring's issue of the *Journal of Cultural Wellness and Pediatric Anthropology*, with the article Post-it–tabbed: "The Urgency of Exposing Cross-Culturally Adopted Children to the Ancestral Cultures of their Biological Parents."

Elias leafed through the pages.

"Two hundred eighteen footnotes," I pointed out.

"You know," Elias said, still taking it in, "they mean well." He grinned. "Urgently."

"Uh-huh," I said. That was the problem. My folks had gotten fixated in a big way. Just after school let out last summer, it had begun with these very serious after-dinner talks at the kitchen table on how I should take pride in my Japanese heritage. It was, they told me, just as valid as their Irish heritage.

I told them then, "I'm fine, get over it." Really, I am. I mean, I'm interested in Japan and stuff, which is why I'm still taking *Nihon'go* as my Asian language elective, but I like a lot of other things, too. Besides, it's not like I'm genetically programmed to worship the emperor, or anything. But when my parents are on a mission to improve me, "I'm fine" is the worst possible thing to tell them.

My mom got a little teary and clasped my hands in hers. "Your ancestors are speaking to you," she said. "We're going to help you hear."

It's been downhill ever since.

"Hey, *ninja*-boy," I said to my little brother, getting back to our project, "Elias and I need to use the computer."

Without looking up, Tim held up a hand, arm bent at the elbow.

At Elias's questioning look, I explained, "He's decided he wants to become a master of stealth and secret death."

"You're kidding," Elias said.

I shook my head. Tim could be a big pain sometimes, but basically he's a good kid. Not that I'd ever tell him that. "My parents have cut him back to an hour of TV a day," I said to Elias. Then, to Tim, "I meant *now!*"

Tim clicked the mouse to disconnect, lifted the scanner cover to take out a sheet of paper, then stood and whirled, his black cape flying behind him. *"Sensei,"* he said to me, "how could you bring *that*" — he pointed at Elias — "to our *dojo?*" Without waiting for an answer, he dashed from the room.

"I didn't know ninjas wore capes," Elias said.

"Don't ask," I replied.

Chapter 6

*S*ecret Messages

Elias

Later, when we'd finished with the science project stuff, Shohei flopped back onto his *tatami* bed. "Since you screwed up my *Titus* idea, I've got a new plan to get you and Honoria together."

"What?" I asked. Sometimes when Shohei's on a roll, it's better to humor him and redirect him later than try to stop him all at once.

"You're going to write her secret letters by e-mail," Shohei said.

"E-mail?" I was appalled.

"Hey, it's the twenty-first century," Shohei replied, deliberately misunderstanding.

"Love letters?"

"We'll set up an e-mail alias and —"

"Is that legal?" I asked. "Isn't it like stalking or something?"

"What are you, the FBI?" Shohei asked. "Look, all you do is set up a couple exchanges, tell her you're an admirer, then move in for the kill."

Then Shohei lay back on the bed and pulled his cap over his eyes.

"What are you doing?" I asked.

He pointed, without looking up. "There's the computer. Start typing."

I sat at his desk, watching the cobra screensaver flash by. I clicked the mouse and opened the word processor. I didn't write a letter. I typed "WHY?" and underneath it made a column of numbers from one to ten:

1. She's smart.
2. She's my friend.
3. She likes things that are creepy, slimy, and have big teeth.
4.
5.
6.
7.
8.
9.
10.

After number 3, I blanked. There was a reason I didn't want to write love letters. I looked at the list, then glanced over my shoulder. Shohei was still lying there, his cap over his face, the Cubs logo mocking me.

I wasn't going to e-mail it anyway.

No. Face-to-face was the only way to go.

I hit "delete" as I thought of number four: *Because to do nothing would be worse.*

Chapter 7

Plagues

Elias

When Honoria and I were in third grade, we went to Vacation Bible School together. That's where I found out that Honoria's favorite part of the Book of Exodus is the plague of locusts. When you get over to her house, you can see why. Her mom's an entomologist who brings her work home. More shelves in the Grob Library — really, a spare bedroom with built-in bookcases — are filled with bottles of bugs than with books. And there are a lot of books.

Since it was Honoria's favorite room, I'd decided it was a good place to tell her that I wanted to move beyond the buddy phase, especially since Shohei didn't seem interested in her. There was the whole problem that she was interested in Shohei. But I was hoping she might get less interested in him if she knew I was interested in her.

The fact that at the moment Honoria was holding a plate of diced cattle hearts and several banana chunks, dripping blood, didn't help the romance factor. Neither did the fifty-gallon tank that housed her two new piranhas, Spot and Fluffy, replacement pets for an iguana named Barbie and a tarantula named Skipper.

"Honoria, I —"

Just then, she turned, still holding the plate, and tripped over her mother's Oriental rug, dumping most of the experimental diet into my lap. I jumped out of my chair, cold cow blood already seeping into my jeans, and the mess slid from my lap onto Honoria's mother's prized rug. Trying to catch my balance, I took a step, squishing a chunk of meat. Honoria gasped and rushed out of the room.

In a moment, she was back with a handful of moistened paper towels. "Here," she handed me some. "I'll pick up the meat. You dab the rug, or Mother will throw both of us in the tank with the killer bees."

I dabbed. Quickly, I ran the paper towel over the top of the rug. Every now and then I glanced up to look at Honoria. She was grabbing at the meat chunks and staring worriedly at where they had fallen, clearly hoping the rug wouldn't permanently stain. Her forehead was a frown, and a couple of strands of hair had fallen over her face.

I thought of brushing away the hair and kissing her, like a normal person. I think I was starting to move in that direction, too, when she announced, "That looks good. I'll get some more bait." Then she strode out the library door.

I rubbed the back of my neck in frustration before realizing my hands were still covered in cow blood. It was okay, I told myself. I was probably better off asking her first. Before I kissed her. Otherwise, she'd probably freak. She might freak anyway.

Honoria returned a moment later with a fresh plate of banana and ground beef heart.

While she resumed her fish training, I decided to try again. "I wanted to tell you —"

"Hey, Eli," Honoria said, holding up a wet plastic leaf. "Do you think it's a problem that Spot and Fluffy are going after the plants in the tank?"

I suppressed a groan and asked, "Are the fish actually eating the leaves?"

Honoria shook her head. "I don't think so. I just found one or two floating on top."

"Then it's probably not a problem," I told her.

Honoria dropped more beef heart and banana into the tank. The fish swam in slow circles but ignored the offering.

One more try, I decided, opening my mouth.

"You know," Honoria interrupted again, "I'm thinking it has to be a gift."

"For the piranhas?" I asked.

"Shohei!" she said, impatiently.

I'd blown my last chance. Still holding the plastic leaf, I watched her scribble some notes on a yellow pad about her heart-eating piranhas.

Honoria

"You know, you're supposed to be wearing your goggles," Goliath Reed told Eli and me in chem lab, with all the self-righteousness of someone who *always* followed the rules, thereby demonstrating beyond a shadow of a doubt that he had no imagination whatsoever.

Eli and I, of course, were not unaware that we were supposed to be wearing our goggles, but they always made Eli's glasses fog up, and even without glasses, the goggles were hot, uncomfortable, obstructed your peripheral vision, and in general made you look like some kind of bubble-eyed space dork.

The lab for the day was how much confectioner's and/or granulated sugar could be dissolved in half a liter of room-temperature water, because Mr. Eden was trying to show how much of the stuff goes into Kool-Aid, or, as he put it, "that revolting beverage probably invented by the Lifetime Employment Division of the American Dental Association." The goggles were not strictly necessary, because there wasn't any actual danger of acids splashing into anyone's eyes, just syrupy water.

Unfortunately, during lab, Mr. Eden prowls the aisles, keeping an eye on things, and he was, in fact, about six feet from Eli when Goliath Reed made his announcement. Something Goliath Reed clearly knew, since he was looking in Mr. Eden's direction.

Mr. Eden instantly came around the lab bench and dragged Eli off his stool by his left ear.

"Ow," Eli said.

"Mr. Brandenburg," Mr. Eden replied. "What. Are. You. Doing?"

Mr. Eden then released Eli's ear, and Eli settled back onto the lab stool.

"I was running the experiment," Eli replied.

Mr. Eden looked at Eli as if he was something stuck to the bottom of one of his polished penny-loafers. "Where, pray tell, are your goggles?"

Behind Mr. Eden, I very quietly put mine on. Mr. Eden

was known to be more strict with some people, and in particular, everyone named Elias Brandenburg, but I wasn't going to take any chances.

"Oh, sorry," Eli said, "but it's just sugar . . ." He pointed out the box. "And I'm wearing my glasses."

I eyed the Bunsen burner and wondered how combustible Mr. Eden's eyebrows were.

"Mr. Brandenburg," Mr. Eden said, "need I remind you that sloppy laboratory procedure is sloppy science?"

"It's just sugar," Eli protested valiantly.

"'Just sugar,'" Mr. Eden repeated. "Mr. Brandenburg, if you do not put on your goggles and cease your cretinous mewling, I will assign you a ten-page report on the metabolic toxicity of refined sugar."

Eli put on his goggles.

"How did you know that the beaker was clean?" Mr. Eden asked, raising an index finger. "Beware of false assumptions!"

Then he strode off, but not before I caught a "I saw you as well, Ms. Grob!"

I watched him go up to the front of the room and write "GOGGLES" in big letters on the whiteboard. The problem with Mr. Eden is that, even when he's right, you don't like him.

Shohei

So I'm at lunch in the school cafeteria eating sushi, again, when Elias comes by with this gift-wrapped box on his tray, next to a plateful of cod nuggets and Tater Tots. "What's that?" I asked.

"A gift," he said, "for that pet of yours. From Honoria. She's got a Student Court meeting."

"Cool," I said, grabbing the box from the tray. I tore open the cardboard, and then, okay, I admit it, I spazzed. These *things* were moving around inside. I dropped the box into my soy sauce, jumping up and knocking over my chair. "It's alive!" I yelled.

"*They're* alive," Elias said, like I was some kind of idiot and it was the most natural thing in the world to be handed a gift box full of squirming rodents.

Three white mice scurried out of the box and raced to the other end of the table, where Freddie M-K was nibbling tofu with her club of animal rights activists.

"Get them!" Elias shouted. "They're heading toward the Murchettes!"

Like I couldn't see that. Elias lunged and managed to grab one of the mice.

Another disappeared onto the floor, and the third somehow got in Freddie's long black hair. She screamed, shaking her head like crazy and waving her hands around.

Then Freddie jumped onto her chair, shouting "Rats!"

while still trying to get rid of Mouse Number Three. By now, the whole cafeteria knew something was going on. Some people stood, some crouched, looking around. Louise Nguyen was clutching a fork like a dagger and, I think, stalking Number Two. Octavian Henderson was next to her, pelting something with Tater Tots. One or two of the *über*cool ignored everything and just kept eating their cod nuggets.

I tried to snatch Mouse Number Three from Freddie's hair. That's when she clobbered me in the eye. Hard. I don't think she meant to; her hands were just flying all over the place.

As I held my hand to my eye, Elias shoved Mouse Number One back into what remained of its box and dived under the table to find the last one. By then, just about everyone was screaming or shouting, either joining the chase or trying to get up onto a chair or a table. One or two teachers appeared, trying to herd everyone out.

"It bit me!" Freddie yelled, clutching at her neck. "It's got rabies! I'm going to die!"

"You're not going to die," I could hear Elias muttering. "But Honoria's definitely going to kill *me*."

Then, someone pulled the fire alarm and Mouse Number Three dashed out of sight. A second later, Vice Principal Harrell's voice came over the loudspeaker: "A fire alarm was pulled in the cafeteria. We do not have a report on whether there is a fire. But everyone, please leave the building. This is not a drill."

That's when I felt my foot come down on something kind of squishy and kind of crunchy.

Then Elias was in front of me. "'It's alive,'" he mimicked. "What did you think Honoria would give Mathilda, a chew toy?"

I shrugged. "Look . . ." I raised my foot to show the squished mouse.

Elias made a face. "We are not going to tell Honoria about that one."

That left just one missing mouse. I crouched down and looked under the now empty tables and chairs. No mouse.

It wasn't my day. First, the snake food got loose in the cafeteria. Next, when I got home after soccer practice, I made the mistake of telling Tim what happened. So he went around all night telling everyone I "got beat up by a girl." The fact that my eye was a gross shade of purple and black with a bit of yellow around the edges didn't help.

Next, I got the lecture from Mom and Dad on how "more effective and persuasive" nonviolence was and how I should "learn from the examples of Mahatma Gandhi and Dr. Martin

Luther King Jr." I explained that Freddie M-K, who was a girl, clocked me in the eye because she was having a fit over a mouse. After that, I got another lecture on how I should not "perpetuate Eurocentric stereotypes about how women are separate from the oneness of Mother Earth."

So, in honor of Mother Earth, I went to my room and fed Mathilda a mouse. While she digested, I got to work on Elias's letter to Honoria. First I rescued his deleted document and figured out that he hadn't actually written a letter. Just some lame list. But he didn't say I shouldn't write one for him. So I did. I even used the thesaurus so I'd sound like Elias. Love letters are harder than they look.

```
Dearest Honoria:
I am not a stalker. I am a fellow Peshtigo
Warrior Penguin. I am writing you this
way because whenever I talk to you, I
feel clumsy and uncoordinated, and I say
ridiculous or frightening things. I admire
you a lot for your intelligence and looks,
and whenever I see you, my heart soars.
Will you be the helium in my balloon?
An Admirer
```

I had just clicked "Send" when the phone rang. It was Elias, calling about the science project, which I had kind of forgotten to work on that day.

"What's up?" he asked.

"Just working on the project," I lied.

"Me, too," he said. "The hypocotyls are beginning to emerge."

"Sounds exciting," I replied, as I logged off my computer.

"The embryonic stems," he explained. "All according to schedule."

"Oh, yeah. Same here," I said. Also according to schedule was his obsessiveness kicking in — he'd complain that his dad was making him do it, or that he was worried about his grades. Really, it's just him. Like last year, when he joined the chess club, he got all these books from the library and played game after game online with his brother Johann Ambrosius and then got kicked off the team for arguing with Mr. Martyniuk about the best way to counter some move named after some old Russian guy.

"Any differences in the control group?"

"Nope."

"Me neither. Probably takes a while."

It was time to stop this. "By the way," I asked, "should you be calling? I mean, aren't we supposed to be going for" — what was it? — "independent confirmation?" Who says I don't pay attention? I held my breath. I was pretty sure I was right. Besides, I didn't want him calling every night to check on me.

"Hmph," he replied.

Honoria

The next day, Eli went with me during study hall to the computer lab in the library, which is the empire of librarian Ruth Talmadge, a former lawyer, sponsor of the Student Court, and a huge White Sox fan who doesn't allow Shohei to wear his Cubs cap in the library. Other than the White Sox thing, which, for the Peshtigo School, is a fairly minor quirk, she's all right.

The computer lab has about twenty top-of-the-line PCs and overlooks the Atrium Garden. I'd gone there to check my e-mail and to do some more research to make sure Spot and Fluffy were, in fact, *Pygocentrus nattereri*. That's what the people at Lincoln Park Pets said, but I've known them to mislabel their crickets *(Gryllus texensis)* and I wanted to make sure they actually knew what they were talking about this time.

"Did Shohei say anything about the mice?" I asked Eli as I logged on. It had taken me a while to pick them out, because I'd wanted something that he would notice that I'd noticed said "Shohei," but not something that made me seem too girlie or pathetic. But I hadn't heard anything from him about it so I was feeling at least a little nervous and possibly borderline terrified.

"He started a riot," Eli replied.

"I know," I said. "We had to reschedule Student Court yesterday. He hasn't said a word to me about it." Not even his usual, "Huh. Weird."

"He probably forgot when Freddie clocked him in the eye," Eli said, while he logged on to his computer.

"How is it?" I asked. "His eye, I mean."

"I've seen worse," Eli replied. "On him, actually."

"She takes tae kwan do," I replied. Freddie and I got along well enough. We weren't like friends who had sleepovers, watched bad movies, made and ate s'mores, giggled over boys, and told each other their innermost secrets, but we could have a healthy debate over small mammal and amphibian dissection in front of the entire school and still be able to speak to each other in public and private with some civility and, sometimes, without shouting.

The only other people in the computer lab were Goliath Reed and Andrea Shaw, Goliath's girlfriend since last year. They were sitting in front of computers at the far corner of the lab, whispering back and forth.

Andrea's on the Student Court. She's got this short red hair that's a shade she calls "titian," she's usually a bit too perky, and she could probably do better than Goliath Reed.

I clicked on an e-mail that was titled "Admirer."

"Oh," I said, after I'd read the message.

"What is it?" Eli looked over from his computer.

"Nothing," I said, looking around my monitor at Goliath and Andrea. He smirked at me and turned away as soon as I glanced at him.

Eli was silent, reading the e-mail.

"I have a secret admirer. How scary is that?" I whispered. "I think it's Goliath Reed. I wouldn't have thought he'd be such a wuss."

"Goliath?" Eli said, too loudly.

Goliath and Andrea were both staring now, frowning. I turned the monitor so Eli could read the rest of the message.

"Are you sure it's Goliath Reed?" Eli asked. "It seems a bit primitive, even for him."

I shook my head, pointing to the last line. "That's definitely a Goliath Reed–level metaphor." I'd heard one too many of them during Student Court. Usually they involved "balancing the scales of justice toward public safety," or some such. And he was looking at me when I read the message. "Who else could it be?"

Eli shook his head and got up, saying, "I just remembered, I have to go."

Elias

Go beat someone up, that is. Okay, I didn't explicitly tell Shohei not to send anything to Honoria, but I had deleted what I'd written. And it wasn't even a letter, anyway. And if he'd *had* to do it, he could've come up with something decent. I know I couldn't come up with anything of my own, but at least I knew better than to try.

But I wasn't able to find Shohei — he wasn't at his locker between classes. I'm almost sure he was trying to hide from me. He didn't say a word during soccer practice, either, so when he got the ball during scrimmage, I stole it from him in what might have been an illegal tackle. Hard.

Shohei was on his feet in an instant. "What is wrong with you?" he yelled.

I was standing a moment later and grabbed his shirt in both hands. "She thinks Goliath Reed is the admirer!" Then I pushed him away.

Shohei's face was blank a moment. "What? Why?"

"Maybe because you can't write love letters?"

He ran a hand through his hair. "Huh. Well, I can fix it. Trust me."

"You'd better," I told him.

Chapter 8

The Easy Way Out

Elias

I'd set up my end of the science project on the worktable in the Archives room. Every night, after piano practice, I checked the CD players to see that they were still running. I took photos of the plants next to a measuring tape. I measured the heights of the stalks, counted the number of leaves and blossoms, and gave them exactly the same amounts of distilled water. It was the way you were supposed to do a science project.

That night I sat in the dark with a set of headphones and listened with the plants to Bach's Brandenburg Concerto No. 6 in B flat major, BWV 1051. Okay, I probably shouldn't have tackled Shohei. The reason I was mad at him for the letter, though, was that now I couldn't tell Honoria how I felt about her, at least not anytime soon.

She was creeped out enough with the idea that Goliath Reed was her secret admirer. If I told her it had been me, and I'd been too chicken to tell her, she'd think I was nuts. Or some sort of freak. Probably both. Definitely both.

♪

Shohei

The thing about science projects is that they're a big pain. You have to do the same thing night after night at the same time and in the same amounts. Water. Feed. Photograph. Measure. Record.

So I got an idea. I figured that if I used our digital camera to take a video every day at the same time I could get a video record with a time stamp. That way, I could go back and use it later for the observations. I could even download the video to my computer for displaying during the judging. That left watering, but I had that figured out, too.

"Tim," I called. No answer.

"Tim-*san*," I called.

"No yelling in the house!" yelled my mom from the kitchen.

A moment later, Tim showed up in the guest room. "I am here, *sensei.*" He bowed. I have to say, the whole ninja act was getting on my nerves. Not that as the only Japanese American O'Leary I owned all things Japanese, but Tim seemed way too into it.

I made him wait a moment.

"I need these plants taken care of," I said. "They need to be watered every night at six o'clock. Starting tomorrow." I showed him how much water to give each plant. "It's very important. The honor of the family depends on it."

Tim pulled his cape around him. "You can count on me, *sensei.*" He bowed low again and dashed off.

Piece of cake.

Elias

The day before the next chem exam, Honoria and I got together in the Grob Library to study. We arranged ourselves at opposite sides of her mother's antique library table, books and papers spread in front of us.

"I have got to ace this exam," I said to Honoria. "I've already blown my lab grade." It counted for twenty-five percent of the total semester grade, and since I was probably running at about seventy percent in lab, depending on the curve, that meant I had almost no leeway if I wanted to get an A in the course.

"You didn't blow your lab grade," Honoria replied, drinking iced tea.

"Mr. Eden said he was taking points off my final grade for the goggles," I said. "My parents will freak if I get a B."

Okay, really, *I'd* freak if I got a B. But Dad probably would, too. I'd never brought home a B in a science class before. Mom and Dad would probably make me get counseling, or test me for drugs, or something infinitely worse.

Honoria and I spent the next hour or so studying stuff like what happens if you mix a carboxylic acid and an ester. At least, Honoria did. I spent most of it sneaking glances at her, and didn't do much concentrating on the text.

"Study break!" Honoria said, after a while. "I've got to show you something. Wait a sec." She jumped up from her chair and left the room for a minute only to return with some paper towels and a plate of her cut-up bananas and beef hearts.

"Watch," Honoria said, plopping one of the combos into the tank. As it sank, Spot circled and swallowed it in one gulp.

"Congrats," I said. "You've done it."

Honoria shook her head. "This is just phase one. And, it turns out, they are, in fact, *Pygocentrus nattereri.* I think. Which means they're known to eat some fruit anyway. I still need to see if I can get them to choose the banana *over* the hamburger."

She dropped one meat chunk and one banana chunk into the tank. Spot immediately clamped onto the heart, but even Fluffy ignored the sinking banana.

"See?" she said with a grimace. "Nothing." Honoria wiped her fingers on a paper towel. "How's your project going?"

"It's not," I replied. "The music's supposed to make the plants grow faster. But it's not working. All my plants are growing at the same rate." I'd even sent an e-mail to big brother Johann Christoph, hoping he had some ideas about what might be wrong, but so far, no response. I knew he was busy after quitting his postdoc in England for his new Internet start-up, but it was still annoying.

Honoria opened her mouth to reply when her mother walked in. Mrs. Grob walked over to one of the bookcases and tilted her head to read the titles on the spines. Every now and then, she'd pull a book out partway, then shove it back.

"Mother, leave," Honoria said, drumming her fingers on the tabletop. "It's just Eli."

Mrs. Grob pulled a book from the shelf, then turned and smiled at Honoria. "I had to grab this." She brandished the book, then left, carefully leaving the door open a crack.

"What was all that about?" I asked Honoria, my voice low.

Honoria grimaced. "All of a sudden Mother's all concerned about me being alone with a boy. I think it's some sort of parental pre-dating complex. But I keep telling her it's not like that. It's just you." Honoria took a sip of iced tea, then went back to her chemistry book.

In the fourth grade, I climbed up on a neighbor's garage to retrieve a softball. I fell off and broke my leg. I blacked out from the pain.

This felt worse.

Chapter 9

Test Anxiety

Honoria

If I hadn't been absolutely certain who the admirer was, I would never have responded to the e-mail. At least not this way:

> I am not your dearest. I wish nothing to do with you. Your attempt to hide your identity is lame and stupid. Bother someone else.

Because I wanted him to know that I knew who he was, I didn't hit "Reply." Instead, I addressed it directly to Goliath Reed's Peshtigo School e-mail account.

Shohei

"Shoot me now," Elias said the next day as we dodged the hallway crowd after the chem exam. "I have never bombed a test that bad."

"You didn't bomb the test," I replied, leaning against my locker. "You always over-study anyway, Mr. Wolf." As in "Boy Who Cried." Elias always complains after an exam that he's bombed it. Usually, he sets the curve. It gets annoying.

He shook his head. "I overslept and didn't get there until twenty minutes into class."

That actually got my attention, but before I could follow up, Freddie M-K and the Murchettes stepped in front of us. They were wearing head-to-toe black, including dolphin-safe lipstick and nail polish. They kind of smelled, too, from their protest against animal fat in soap.

"Sign this pledge," Freddie said, shoving a clipboard at Elias. The notebook paper had about ten signatures on it, including Goliath Reed's.

I read over Elias's shoulder.

We, the undersigned, are opposed to animal experimentation in all forms whatsoever and, as participants in the Gloriana Biddulph Memorial Science Fair, do hereby pledge that we will not, under any circumstances whatsoever, take part in such acts of barbarism and cruelty.

"This is the most insanely stupid thing I've ever heard of," Elias told Freddie, thrusting the clipboard back at her.

Freddie opened a folder and held up a photo.

"This is what the cosmetics companies do to bunnies!" she exclaimed. She held up another. "This is what the auto companies do to monkeys!" A third. "This is what jet engine manufacturers do to geese!"

A couple of passers-by made faces but bolted before Freddie could get to them. That's when Elias lost it.

"I *like* animal experiments," he said, spitting out the words. "I *like* mascara testing on rabbits. I *like* crash-testing rhesus monkeys. And I *love* the goose cannon!"

"As long as you thaw them first," I said, grinning. Freddie and Elias both stared. "The geese," I said. "They're, like, already dead, right?"

Freddie sniffed. "Monsters!" she called, then swept away with her group.

"I like veal, too!" Elias called after her. "And steak! Especially chicken-fried steak!"

The flow of students gave us a little extra space after that. We were both silent a moment, while Elias glared after Freddie.

"I thought chicken-fried steak made you gag," I said finally, not sure what had gotten into Elias.

Elias threw his backpack into his locker. "Let me put it to

you this way: We are not going to sign anything that accuses Honoria of murder for trying to find out if you can make a piranha become a vegetarian. The save-the-animals people should applaud her efforts. Besides, do you think Honoria would really do anything to hurt Spot and Fluffy? Especially after what her house sitter did to Barbie and Skipper?"

"Oh, yeah," I said. Honoria had been upset for weeks. Until she got the piranhas, anyway. "Hadn't thought about that." I shrugged. "Freddie's kind of cute, though, don't you think?"

Elias gave me a kind of glare but just said, "Yeah, well, the black lipstick's creepy." Then he slammed his locker door shut and stalked off.

Honoria

The sole item on the Office of the Public Defender's agenda for the day was whether to drop Josh Patel from the Office because of the incident in the Garden with the root beer, or whether we should merely censure him.

"Anything else?" I asked, looking around the conference room, after forty-five minutes of indecision. Two of the other student defense attorneys shook their heads, or said no, and exited. The only good thing about the meeting was that we had managed to grab the best conference room — the one on the southwest corner of the building with the view over the old pier terminal mall toward Ogden Slip and downtown.

Andrea Shaw didn't follow the others out. She wasn't that bad, despite the Goliath Reed relationship. She performed adequately as a student defender and had a fairly good record. "Stay away from my boyfriend," she said. She said it calmly, as if it was a matter of only minor importance.

"I'm not interested in your boyfriend," I replied, as I felt my face turn red.

"That's exactly what you'd say if you were," Andrea said, marching off.

Elias

Shohei and I were at the back of the team bus after our soccer game in Evanston. Shohei had scored a goal, giving him the best scoring percentage on the team. We'd only lost by three this time, which meant that we'd only been outscored, on average, 4.5 to 1, per game. Coach Swindler's postgame pep talk still echoed in the bus, but my mind wasn't really on the game.

"Have you figured out yet what to do about the e-mail to Honoria?" I asked.

60

"I'm working on it," Shohei replied.

That was Shohei-ese for "I have no idea, but maybe something will come to me."

It meant, though, that I had a little while before I needed to worry about what he was going to do next, so I went on to the second thing.

Shohei had refused to take my live conduct-the-experiment calls after the first week. Then, it hadn't really mattered, because I had my brother Christoph's results and I expected mine to show the same thing: that the baroque music would cause the plants to grow better. But that still wasn't happening. So now, it was looking like Shohei's results might make a difference. What's more, I hadn't gotten a reply from Christoph in over a week and the science fair was only three weeks away.

"How's your project?" I asked.

Shohei leaned back against the seat. "Fine," he said.

"How much of a growth differential are you seeing? Any reaction to the bagpipes? What about the control group?"

"Chill," Shohei said, raising his voice above the din of the Nerf ball game going on in the front of the bus. "It's just a science fair."

"Yeah," I said, "but we've still got to do it right."

"Why are you so uptight?" Shohei asked. "You didn't even want to do it."

"As long as we're doing it," I answered, "we should do it right."

He stared at me. "And?"

"And if I get a B my dad will kill me."

"No, he won't," Shohei said. "Last year Jake got a C in calculus, and he lived."

"I am not Jake," I said. Okay, I was *expected* to get A's but it wasn't demanded. But I could just see it: my dad would propose a test of his own to determine if I actually knew the subject (which was what he would say actually mattered) and make sure there wasn't some statistical aberration in the questions or grading curve. My mom, on the other hand, would tell me that it was okay, and that she had succeeded quite nicely and had a fulfilling career, thank you very much, without knowing anything at all about the Second Law of Thermodynamics. Then she would ask me if I had finished my piano practice for the day.

The thing was, unlike Shohei, I liked being one of the Smart Ones. I liked always doing well and getting A's. And I hated looking stupid.

The stray Nerf ball shot our way, and Shohei snagged it. "The experiment's fine. The plants don't like the bagpipes, they don't care about the waterfall, and they love the harpsichord." He threw the ball back up front. "Happy now?"

I answered, "Yeah." But really, I wasn't.

Chapter 10

E-mail

Elias

That evening, I sent another e-mail to Number One Son, Johann Christoph, still in England, but this time, to his new e-mail address at the start-up:

```
Earth to Christoph —
Still no growth differential. Shohei's
running the same experiment, though, and
says his results match yours. What
gives?
— Elias
```

Chapter 11

Oops

Honoria

"It's not going to work," Goliath Reed told me the next day after yet another administrative meeting for Student Court. We were the only ones left in the library conference room.

I was going to have to get out of these meetings earlier, I decided.

"What's not going to work?" I asked, having no idea what he was talking about and not really caring that much, either.

"That e-mail," he said.

I froze. I did not want to have this conversation with Goliath Reed.

Then he continued, "Whatever weird psych-out game you and your friends are playing, it's not going to work. I know you really want to win the science fair."

He was totally, completely serious.

"Sure," I replied. "Whatever you say."

He shrugged, then turned to leave.

As he was opening the door, I called, "Wait." When Goliath glanced back, I asked, "What is your science project on this year?"

He smirked. "Which brand of battery lasts the longest."

Another commercial, consumer project.

I did not scream.

"It was the most peculiar conversation I've ever had," I told Eli. I'd called him later that night and filled him in on my talk with Goliath Reed. "So what do you think I should do? I mean, he was all 'You're getting all underhanded and every-thing' but he didn't actually say he wasn't the admirer."

"Why do you have to do anything?" Eli asked. "Sounds like he's giving up."

"That's just it," I said. "I don't know that he is. That whole big dumb 'Let's not play games' could just be an act."

"Yeah," Eli said, but it didn't sound like he meant it.

Chapter 12

The Rites of Grading

Elias

The Returning of the Exams is an exercise in public humiliation. Usually, though, I am not the humiliated. On paper, it sounds harmless: the instructors call names and read scores. Aloud. To the whole class. It's a Peshtigo School tradition. Some of the psycho alum parents even insist on it, especially the lawyers. It's supposed to build character, or something.

Most of the teachers don't do it anymore. Others just post the grades on the bulletin board in the cafeteria hallway, also known as the "Wailing Wall."

Mr. Eden really gets into it. He spends the first half of class reciting names and scores, from high to low, usually with some sarcastic remarks. He spends the rest of the class going over answers, explaining in detail why you were an idiot for not having gotten them right.

The particular rite in question took place in one of the chem lecture rooms, connected to the lab. Each is the same: four tiers of those chairs with the one-sided desk platforms that — according to Honoria — discriminate against left-handed people. A table with a lectern for the speaker was up front, along with four of those liftable whiteboards.

When I got to class, Mr. Eden was writing the class grade distribution on one of the whiteboards. After the bell rang, Mr. Eden took up his place behind the lectern.

I knew I had done badly on the chem test. When I sat down to take it, twenty minutes late, everything I'd studied the night before, which wasn't much, had leaked out. I'd hoped I hadn't gotten the lowest score on the exam. What I had not expected was —

"Mr. Brandenburg," enunciated Mr. Eden, smoothing his fringe of hair. "Do you know what the 'Monkey Score' is?"

"Yes," I said quietly, feeling my face turn red and glancing toward the exit. Five seats separated me from the door. Two rows in front, one in back, and no easy way out.

Mr. Eden continued, "It's the score you get on a multiple-choice test if the distribution of answers is truly randomized and if you fill in C for every question."

Those who were glad to be free from Mr. Eden's attention, and those were just jerks, laughed. Goliath Reed, who was in the seat in front of Honoria and me, laughed the loudest.

Honoria kicked him. Part of me was glad she was on my side. The other part of me was remembering how she'd said "It's just you" in her library.

Mr. Eden went on, "There were one hundred questions on your exam, each with four possible answers. Your score," he paused, enjoying himself way too much, "was a twenty-four." As Mr. Eden flipped the exam paper toward me, Goliath ducked.

The exam paper landed in my lap.

"Try to study next time," Mr. Eden said, "or hie thee to the Lincoln Park Zoo for a monkey to take the test for you."

Chapter 13

Turning Japanese

Shohei

Wednesday night, Tim and I were on stools at the kitchen island while my mom was at the sink deveining shrimp for the tempura. It was a family favorite, even before the Japan effort. I was shredding carrots while Tim fidgeted and grabbed at the carrot pile.

"Tim!" I yelled at him as he stuffed a third handful into his mouth.

"Tim, don't eat the carrots," my mom said without looking our way.

Slowly, Tim spit out the carrots, to splotch onto the countertop.

"Gross," I said.

"Tim, clean that up," my mom said, again without turning around.

Before she got any further, we heard the key in the lock.

"Daddy's home!" Tim shouted and ran off.

I looked at the clock on the microwave: 6:30. He was home early. My dad's a lawyer at a big firm on LaSalle Street. He almost never got home by 6:30.

"Umph," we heard from down the hall, a sign that Tim had connected.

A moment later, my dad walked in, carrying Tim piggyback. After he said "hi" and my parents smooched, he took off with Tim down the hall.

When my dad came back, he had changed into one of his Chicago Triathlon T-shirts and orange and blue University of Illinois shorts.

"Hey, kid," Dad said as he took off my Cubs hat. "When's the game Saturday?" My parents have had season tickets and have been making day trips down to Champaign for Illini football since they graduated. U of I loses a lot, but it's kind of fun.

I shook my head. "They're at Minnesota."

"Saturday we open the patio," Mom reminded my dad. Our patio had been redone as part of the same remodeling that had taken over my room, but it took a while longer.

"And," Mom continued, "I was going to show Shohei how to do *ikebana*."

"Oh, right," Dad said, before he focused on me. "What's this Tim says about him watering the plants for your project?"

That could be trouble. I didn't think Tim would tell. "Um, he wanted to," I said. "I didn't make him or anything."

Dad looked at Tim. "Tim," Dad asked, "do you want to water Shohei's plants?"

Tim nodded and said proudly, "For the honor of the family."

My parents traded some silent communication.

"He can do it as long as he wants to," Mom said. She pointed at me, "but *only* as long as he wants to. He is not your slave."

"Of course not," I replied, innocent-like.

"Just make sure you remember that," Mom said. "Now, the only other thing is, who do you want over for the patio celebration?"

I was kind of puzzled. "Are we talking big party, here, 'cause I thought those were out after last year with the carpet and all . . ."

"We were thinking maybe Elias and Honoria," Dad said in a hurry.

"'Kay," I replied. They, at least, would be on my side.

So, later that night, I called Elias and conferenced in Honoria.

"I need your help," I said.

"What's wrong?" Honoria asked.

"Saturday is the unveiling of the new patio," I replied, "and —"

"You want us to cut the ribbon?" Elias asked.

"Funny. No. I need you guys there for the *ikebana*."

"Is that a type of food?" Honoria wanted to know. I heard Elias laughing.

"It's the art of Japanese flower arranging," I replied. My mother, it turned out, had been taking university extension lessons. "My mom wants to demonstrate. It's supposed to be, I don't know, Zen or something, which is weird because last time I checked, we were Catholic."

"You want us there to protect you," Elias asked. He was still laughing.

"I'll be there," Honoria answered.

"Me, too," Elias said.

Chapter 14

Garden in the ʃky

Honoria

I hadn't been over to the O'Learys' since Shohei's last birthday party and the incident with the chunky peanut butter and the Berber carpeting, which could have been a lot worse if we hadn't found out on the Internet how to clean it up without leaving a permanent stain before Mrs. O'Leary noticed. We would have gotten away with it, too, if Tim hadn't blabbed.

When I got up to their elevator foyer, Mrs. O'Leary was there, wearing a gorgeous black-and-gold kimono. She looked like something out of *Madama Butterfly.*

As soon as Eli arrived, Mrs. O'Leary took us all out to see their new rooftop patio.

Last year, there had been four neatly tended beds of flowers and native prairie grasses, and a small greenhouse Mrs. O'Leary called an *orangerie,* for orange and lime trees, "inspired by the one at Versailles itself." These had been removed, donated, I found out later, to the Lincoln Park Conservatory, and had been replaced with several yards of raked pea gravel and three large, gray boulders.

"How did you get the rocks all the way up here?" Eli asked.

Shohei knocked on one. "Fiberglass," he said.

"It's a Zen rock garden," Mrs. O'Leary explained, "modeled after the one at Ryoanji Temple in Kyoto, Japan. It's for Shohei to have a place to meditate."

An icy breeze blew in from the lake.

"Not today," Shohei muttered.

Mrs. O'Leary led the way back inside. When she was out of earshot, I turned to Eli. "Pay up," I said, holding out my hand.

He handed me a five. At Shohei's puzzled look, he explained, "I bet her your parents were putting in a koi pond."

"I'm so glad," Shohei said, "you guys think it's funny."

"I think it's sweet," I said. Eli did a double take.

Shohei grabbed me by the arms, "Okay, you evil space alien," he said, "return the real Honoria immediately!"

I blushed. "Well, I do," I said, trying not to be flustered

that he was touching me. "And your parents *are* Peshtigo alums, after all. You can't *not* expect some insanity."

Shohei let go, shaking his head.

When we got to the O'Leary dining room, we found the table covered in newspapers and *ikebana* vases, both tall and short; a bunch of stem holders that resembled miniature beds of nails and which we were informed were called *kenzan;* several pairs of scissors; and at least a dozen chunks of Styrofoam. Also piled in the center of the table was an assortment of branches and flowers and stems that looked like they had been culled from the Atrium Garden, and which Mrs. O'Leary identified for us as including alocasia, anthurium, lady's mantle, blue fantasy, glory lily, and smokegrass.

Mrs. O'Leary sat at the head of the table. I sat next to Shohei, with Eli across from us. Tim was there too, even though he was supposed to be getting ready to go out for pizza with a friend from kindergarten and his mother, I think, but he was hovering around and, every time Shohei would place a branch, Tim would try to steal it. Eli and I thought it was pretty hysterical, especially since Tim was still in his ninja cape. We kept glancing across the table and trying not to laugh at each other or Shohei.

Every now and then, Mrs. O'Leary would tell Tim not to play with the scissors.

There were, Mrs. O'Leary told us, two kinds of *ikebana*,

moribana and *nageire,* and we were doing the *moribana,* the kind where you fix the stems in place in the needle holders, the other variety apparently being too advanced for us, or requiring a more contemplative spirit, or some such. The branch of pear brush I put together with some baby's breath and anthurium were praised by Mrs. O'Leary as "suggesting the feel of a boisterous, warm breeze." Eli's greenbrier, smokegrass, and spray mums had "a bold chicness, evocative of a sweet scent."

Shohei's orange flare cosmos, glory lily, blazing star, and fennel were just a mess. It wasn't his fault, though; Tim kept running off with the smilax.

Finally, Tim reached for a yellow oncidium flower as Shohei was trying to place one in his needle holder. Shohei showed some good reflexes, though, and caught Tim's arm, as Tim was making a break for it.

"Hey, ninja-boy," Shohei said, "Don't you have someplace to be?"

Mrs. O'Leary nodded, looking at the grandfather clock. "Mrs. Alpert should be here with Isaac in a few minutes."

She got up, took Tim by the hand and led him away.

As she was taking him down the hall, Tim said, "Mom, how come Shohei gets to do all the cool stuff?"

"Yeah, that's what I'd like to know," Shohei muttered, but his mom was out of earshot.

Chapter 15

Life and Death

Shohei

Each night, at 6:15, Tim had been coming to my room and announcing, "*Sensei,* the plants have been watered. For the honor of the family." After that, he'd bow and back out of my room. The night after the *ikebana* fest, he didn't appear. At around a quarter to seven, I went into the guest bedroom for the first time in a while.

The plants were gone.

The pots were still there, and the bases of the stems, and probably the roots. But everything else was gone. Chopped off. Taken away. Ruined. Elias was going to kill me.

"Tim!" I yelled. No answer. "Tim!" I ran to his bedroom and threw open the door. Tim was lying on his stomach on his twin bed, watching a *Batman* video.

"What happened to the plants?" I demanded.

"Ikebana!" He pointed to his windowsill.

I walked over. The dried plant corpses were sculpted into a freakish display, stuck together with glue and pipe cleaners. Every last one of them.

"You," I whispered to Tim, "are in so much trouble."

He ran.

After I duct-taped Tim to his bed, I went back to the guest bedroom, and sat down to think.

It wasn't that bad, I decided. I still had, more or less, the entire project on MPEG video.

I grabbed the video camera from the nightstand, and hit "Play." The video of the project swept by on the little LCD display. It was okay until about a couple weeks ago, with one or two other gaps. Maybe more. I'd only taken the video about three or four times a week. If that. The thing that caught my eye, though, was that there was no difference in the heights of any of the plants. They all looked about the same. Slightly wilted.

Something was wrong.

I grabbed a tape measure and opened the door to Tim's room. He was still stuck to the bed, though he'd gotten a foot free. I measured the dead plants Tim still had on his windowsill. Yep, they were all about the same size.

Very weird.

I went back to my room and opened Elias's *Big Book of Experimental Procedures* to the appendix that had a copy of his brother Christoph's final report, to double-check. Christoph had had four sets of plants, same as us: a control group that got no music; Group A that got baroque; Group B that got the Niagara Falls (Christoph's report called it "therapeutic white noise"); and Group C that got the bagpipes. According to Christoph, the Group A baroque plants should have shown about a twenty to twenty-five percent improvement in growth compared to the control group that got none, and about twelve percent more than the others. In other words, music helped plants grow. Especially the baroque stuff.

I'd been telling Elias I was getting the same results that Christoph had. But as far as I could tell, my experiment had been going wrong from the start.

Chapter 16

Not Goliath Reed

Honoria

I pulled my bedroom drapes closed so the sun wouldn't glare on my computer screen and logged on to check messages. There was only one that wasn't spam, with "Not Goliath Reed" in the subject heading.

```
Honoria —
I am not Goliath Reed.
Still Your Admirer.
```

I grabbed my phone and began to dial.

"This is getting ridiculous," I said when Eli picked up on his cell phone. "Either my admirer is an idiot or thinks I am." If he was an idiot, I wouldn't want to date him. If he thought I was an idiot, I still wouldn't want to date him.

"What's wrong?" Eli asked.

I read him the message. A roaring sound came out of the handset.

"Sorry — the El just went by. I'm outside on Eastwood walking Beastmaster VII. All I caught was 'I am not Goliath Reed.'"

"That's all there is," I told him, leaning back and adjusting the cushion on my wooden swivel chair.

"Maybe that's all he had to say," Eli said.

"Why would Goliath tell me it wasn't him in an e-mail if he didn't tell me it wasn't him in person?"

"What?"

I put my feet up on my bed. "It doesn't make sense for Goliath to send me this." I picked up a pen and began doodling circles on a notepad. "Maybe it's not him."

"That's what I've been —"

"Wait a minute!" I sat up. It had to be someone who knew I thought it might be Goliath Reed. Plus, I had only told one person. I couldn't believe I hadn't thought of it before. "It's *you*, Eli, isn't it?"

Chapter 17

Not Me

Elias

I nearly dropped the phone. It was sort of good that she didn't seem grossed out by the idea it was me, but I was also sort of horrified she thought I wrote *those* messages.

"I . . . I . . . ," I just stuttered.

"You're the only one I told I still thought it was Goliath Reed."

I stopped in the middle of the sidewalk. Beastmaster VII pulled on his end of the leash. I tried to think of something to say. She couldn't find out *this* way. "I would never write that bad. Badly. Whatever." Aaagh!

"No," Honoria agreed. "Unless you were pretending . . ."

"Pretending . . ."

Before I could process where that was going, she said, "Wait a second! You're doing this for *Shohei* aren't you? That's so sweet!"

"No!" I said. "I'm not doing it for Shohei. I'm not doing it for anyone." This was not going at all the way I wanted it to.

"You're sending Admirer letters to him too, aren't you? That was your plan, right?"

Not my plan. Shohei's. "I didn't have a plan," I said. "It's not me."

"Hold on, though," she went on. "How could you let me make a fool of myself with Goliath? You knew I thought it was him!"

"It wasn't me!" I said.

This was bad, I figured, taking a deep breath, but it was fixable. She had it all backward. I just had to tell her the truth — that Shohei was impersonating me. Anonymously.

"No, wait!" I said. "You've got it all —"

"Well, don't you dare tell Shohei I know. I want it to be a surprise for him."

Click.

"— wrong."

♪

Shohei

So I was trying to figure out how to handle Elias and my project when my dad opened my bedroom door. "We're having the Eichbaums over for dinner Saturday night," Dad said from the doorway of my room. "So no Illini game."

"Do I have to?" I asked. My parents' dinner parties are not that exciting. Okay, I wasn't hugely disappointed about the game. Illinois was playing Michigan, so they'd probably lose. Besides, mid-November would be cold and probably rainy. Maybe even snow. But it was fun going with Dad, even though he sometimes got a bit too into the game.

My dad laughed. "Yes," he said. "Do you good."

I sighed, but marked the event in my Palm Pilot. The Eichbaums had just moved into our building a couple weeks ago. They had two daughters — Megan and Mallory — adopted from China. I'd seen them in the elevators with their parents, but never spoken to them. Megan was my age, and was going to the local public elementary school until she heard back from the Peshtigo School. Mallory was a couple years older, in high school at Lane Tech.

Normally, I might've wanted to meet them. But I knew the only reason they'd been invited was because my parents wanted me to bond on an adopted-Asian-American-kid level with Megan and Mallory. Don't believe for a second Mom and Dad threw dinner parties for every new building resident. No, this was for my benefit.

I was just deciding I couldn't take any more when my dad popped back in.

"Sorry, I forgot," he said. "Starting this Saturday afternoon — your mother's signed you up for bonsai classes."

"I'm not going," I said.

"You're going," Dad replied, shutting the door again.

Chapter 18

Affairs of ∫cience

Honoria

The science fair was organized as a morning-to-evening event, which Eli called a waste of a perfectly good day of television (even though it was a school day and he didn't really watch much TV anyway), while Shohei said he'd take any excuse to avoid going to classes, even if it wasn't the best one ever. In the morning, participants set up their projects and got to check out the competition. In the afternoon, the judges would circulate and, finally, in the evening, parents and the rest of the public would attend to view and, sometimes, be educated.

My mother, who had driven both Eli and me because Eli had offered his old red wagon to help with my fish tank, dropped us off in front of the gym and then, in the first sign that it was going to be a very long day, we found out that nobody had unlocked the gym doors. Seven or eight people in jackets or raincoats snaked in a line with their projects from the top of the stairs of the gym to the sidewalk. I didn't see Shohei, but Freddie and a couple of the Murchettes were marching around, carrying placards telling us to SAVE THE BUNNIES!

"Don't they have classes?" my mother asked.

"Mr. Fresnel signed them out," I guessed. "Freddie's his pet."

With my mother making disapproving noises behind the wheel, Eli and I unloaded the minivan, lining our projects up on the sidewalk.

My mother waved good-bye and drove off, cutting in front of a honking trolley-bus, and we headed into line behind Goliath Reed and his stuffed Energizer bunny.

"Watch my stuff," Goliath ordered as he went off around the building. I will say this for him — he was the only one there smart enough to try to find someone with a key.

I grabbed our poster boards and display materials, and Eli pulled the wagon with my travel fish tank. I'd only brought Spot, because I didn't want to crowd both him and Fluffy in the small carrier.

As we got in line, Freddie blocked our way. "Save the bunnies!" she shouted. "Be nice to mice! Germs are people, too!"

I was not in the mood for a debate. "Move," I told her, gesturing with the poster boards.

"Are you running an animal experiment?" Freddie asked. "Killing frogs or something?"

"Training piranhas," I said, "to prefer bananas. The cattle were already dead."

"How," Freddie said, waving her placard, "do you justify cruelty to poor, defenseless creatures?"

I laughed and pulled the towel off the tank. "Stick your hand in," I said, smiling, "but don't say I didn't warn you." I clicked my teeth.

That was when Freddie and the Murchettes pulled out balloons filled with red paint. "This," Freddie proclaimed, holding one high, "represents the blood of every animal sacrificed in inhumane experiments!" She spun around and threw it at Dionne Johnson and her rat-versus-guinea pig maze project. Other Murchettes flung paint balloons everywhere, even toward people with projects that didn't involve animals. Projecteers began yelling as paint splattered them and their science projects. Suzanne Sverdlov, whose mom was a federal judge, threatened to sue.

Freddie grabbed another paint balloon from her backpack and raised it toward me.

"Try it," I said.

As Freddie drew back to throw, Eli grabbed at her arm, knocking the balloon out of her hand and making her lose her balance. Some of the paint splashed onto our poster boards, but most of it drenched Goliath Reed's boxes. Freddie followed it, flailing, and landed on a box of Goliath's batteries.

That was when Goliath Reed himself came back.

"Hi," I said. "Did you find a key?"

Elias

The Union of Students Concerned About Cruelty to Animals scattered before Goliath, which allowed the rest of us to get into the gym to set up our projects. The science fair was in the second biggest gym, the one the size of a couple basketball courts side-by-side and used mostly for volleyball and wrestling.

A twenty-foot-tall mural of Phlogiston, the Warrior Penguin, loomed over everything. There were about sixty projects, each getting about twelve square feet of display space.

The projects would all be judged on appearance, execution, clarity, and methodology.

I was nervous, which sort of surprised me. Dad had forced me into doing the project but it had been — not fun, exactly — but better than I expected. And, there was the chance I'd win. A good chance, I thought, which would also really help my chem grade.

Because my dad and who-knows-how-many-other parents had refused to take on the job, Mr. Eden himself was to be the chief judge. His two sub-judges were from the advanced placement classes at the Peshtigo School's College Preparatory High School Division. The guy was sort of skinny, with a beige sweater vest and matching trousers that made him look like a bratwurst with arms. The girl, on the other hand, wore faded overalls with a long-sleeve tie-dyed T-shirt, rose-tinted glasses, and carried a leather day planner over her shoulder like a weapon.

Shohei wasn't there yet.

The pair of sub-judges were walking around with clipboards and asking Honoria pointed questions about her experimental procedure.

"Then," Honoria said, "I tried to wean them from the beef hearts to the banana, exclusively." She pointed to one of her photographs of the training. It was the one with the six blobs of banana resting in the tank gravel while the fish swam above.

She never had been able to persuade Spot and Fluffy to embrace vegetarianism.

"Why didn't you simply stop feeding one of the piranhas altogether?" Mr. Eden asked, peering into the tank and tapping the glass.

"Yeah," Bratwurst guy chimed in, "if they'd been hungry enough, they'd have eaten the banana."

"First," Honoria said, straightening to glare at the guy, "I was not about to starve Spot and Fluffy. Second: we already know that *P. nattereri* are omnivores. Third: I wasn't trying to just get them to eat bananas, but to *prefer* bananas over meat." She referred them back to her Statement of Inquiry, and then started talking something about limited sample sizes and replied to a question on whether her hypothesis was properly falsifiable.

"Why did you do it in the first place?" the girl asked. "Who cares whether piranhas want to eat bananas?"

I didn't hear Honoria's answer, because I'd just spotted Shohei at the end of the aisle.

"Sorry I'm late." Shohei rushed up, carrying a length of poster board, his laptop computer slung over one shoulder, and a brown expandable file folder. "Can you help me get set up?"

"Sure," I said, glancing up to see Mr. Eden lifting the lid off the tank. "Where are your plants?"

"Umm," Shohei said, sort of grimacing, "about that. I don't have any. Tim killed them all to make an *ikebana* project and —"

"What?" I asked, stunned. "When? *Why didn't you tell me?*"

"Well," he began.

"Never mind right now," I said, trying not to freak out too much. "Let's get set up fast."

We hurried to set up his poster board, arrange his records, and boot up his computer.

"Mr. Brandenburg," Mr. Eden said. "You are next. Do enlighten us."

I gave Shohei a glare, then calmly launched into my explanation, without even glancing at my notes.

As soon as I had finished the background, Mr. Eden started questioning, "You essentially copied your brother Johann Christoph's experiment?"

"Only the apparatus," I said, trying to ignore the other judges hovering behind Mr. Eden, and feeling a bit disoriented and a bit angry. I mean, I had told him that before he'd approved the project. If he'd had a problem with it, why didn't he bring it up then? "But, I conducted the actual experiment independently in an attempt to verify —"

"Yet you failed to obtain the same results as Christoph?" Mr. Eden asked.

I swallowed. Johann Michael claimed Mr. Eden was the

best teacher at the Peshtigo School *because* he was impossible and demanding, but Johann Michael didn't say that until after he'd graduated and moved thousands of miles away to go to college in Hawaii.

"I was unable to confirm that music will affect the growth rate of the Wisconsin Fast Plant," I finally managed to say, standing straight.

"And to what do you attribute your failure?" Mr. Eden asked.

"There are three possibilities," I said, taking a breath and dabbing at a spot of red paint on a corner of my poster board. "First, Christoph's process was flawed. Second, my process was flawed. Third, neither was flawed, but these particular plants are tone-deaf."

Okay, it was a bad joke.

"And which possibility do you think is most likely?" Mr. Eden asked, while the laptop monitor displayed a slide show of the progress of the experiment. "Mr. Brandenburg," he continued, too quickly for me to answer, "your display is very stylish. I think you will find, however, that in science, we prize substance over style."

Then he walked over to bother Shohei. He turned to the last page of Shohei's final report. One glance.

"Even Mr. O'Leary thinks you got it wrong," Mr. Eden declared, leading his minions away to the next aisle of projects.

Mr. O'Leary thinks I got it wrong, I thought. The same Mr. O'Leary who killed his plants and didn't bother to bring them to the fair. I leaned back on my project table and looked over at Shohei. He was looking cornered and trapped, and a little like a small rodent.

"Oh, no," he said.

"What?" I asked, confused.

"Um," he glanced at his feet. "I did something wrong, too. Before Tim killed the plants, there was no difference in how my groups did."

"What do you mean?" I asked. "What about your data? The pictures?"

"I copied from Christoph's final report." He looked at me, waiting for me to say something.

"Are you insane?" I asked.

It was cheating.

It meant his "official" results were bogus, and his real results confirmed *mine*, and — most of all — that probably meant Christoph's results were off. It meant my supposedly genius brother, who was Mr. Eden's ultimate teacher's pet of all time, had somehow done the experiment wrong.

Shohei started to say something, then paused. My tone, maybe. Or expression.

I'd gone out of my way to let Shohei do part of my project. Killing the plants was one thing. As long as he had the data, it wasn't fatal. But he hadn't even told me. And then, he completely undercut me in front of Mr. Eden. And Shohei knew I wasn't getting a difference in my plant growth either, and what made him decide Christoph got it right and I didn't?

I stormed off, leaving Shohei standing in front of his project.

Chapter 19

∫cores

Honoria

The rest of the day between the end of the judging and the evening session and medal announcements seemed to take about a week, even though I thought I'd aced Mr. Eden's questioning. The other two judges hadn't asked anything difficult, and they seemed to like my display and think that my project was innovative and that piranhas were way cooler than Goliath Reed's batteries. So I was feeling pretty optimistic about my chances.

An hour before we were supposed to leave to see the science fair results, my mother got an emergency call from the bug lab about some new samples. She was very apologetic about not being able to go to the fair, but I didn't mind too much, because if I won, we could celebrate later. If not, I didn't want her there, trying to cheer me up. I ended up going with Elias and his father instead.

I was a little nervous about it, and not just because of the science fair. Dr. Brandenburg isn't very talkative and doesn't really speak so much as make pronouncements. I don't think he likes me much. Eli says he just hasn't gotten over the time I played the *Cats* soundtrack on the Brandenburg house speakers when Dr. Brandenburg was working on his annual budget report.

But when he and Eli picked me up, Dr. Brandenburg said "hello" and helped me load the tank, with Fluffy this time because it only seemed fair, into the backseat of the Mercedes. After that, we were silent the rest of the way to school. Eli was a lot more quiet than usual. I wondered how his morning judging had gone. It seemed best not to ask until his father wasn't around.

As soon as we got out of the Mercedes in the school parking lot, we heard singing. "We Shall Overcome" rose into the autumn night from the steps of the West Gym. The singers — Freddie and the Murchettes — were dressed in furry costumes: a gorilla, a raccoon, a couple of mice, and an elephant, even though elephants aren't furry. Freddie herself was dressed as a cat and carrying an I'M NICE TO MICE sign.

"They're a little flat," Dr. Brandenburg remarked, a few minutes later, as we approached the protesters.

A couple of the Murchettes stepped in front of us, shouting, "Free the fish!"

"Remove yourselves," Dr. Brandenburg said, in what Eli calls his dad's "scare-the-undergraduates" tone.

They removed themselves.

"Clearly," Dr. Brandenburg added, "the Peshtigo School is not what it once was."

When we reached the gym, I restrained myself from rushing ahead to check my score, and let Eli pull the wagon with Fluffy's tank to my project display. When we got there, the medal was hanging from my display cardboard. Silver. Second place.

"Hey," Eli said. "Second place is good, too."

I grabbed my medal and walked up the aisle to where Goliath Reed's project sat, looking like it had corporate sponsorship. Attached to the red-paint-dabbed Energizer bunny was the gold medal. When I turned around, I bumped into Goliath Reed himself. He smiled and held up four fingers. Four science fairs in a row.

I walked past him without saying a word.

Elias

Honoria ran off. I would've followed, but she ran into the girls' locker room. I waited a bit, hoping she'd come out, hoping there was something I could do to make her feel better.

After I'd read all the announcements on the bulletin board outside the locker room, and she still hadn't come out, I wandered back over to my project, where Mrs. O'Leary was looking back and forth between Shohei's display and mine. I didn't see Shohei anywhere, but I didn't want to see him anyway.

Neither of us had medaled, but after the morning inquisition, I wasn't expecting to. White participation certificates sat on the table in front of our projects.

Then I saw my score sheet. It was worse than I'd thought possible. With my lab grade, my F on the exam, and now this, I was probably looking at a D+. I'd never gotten even a C before. It was humiliating. Brandenburgs did not get D's. I folded the sheet and pocketed it before Dad saw it, I hoped.

He didn't seem to notice. He was busy playing with my time-lapse display of the plant growth process. "I may need you to work on my next grant proposal," he said.

It was a compliment, I think.

As Dad continued his examination of my project, I stood still, waiting for his final assessment. With a forefinger, he touched one of the red paint splotches the Murchettes had left.

Then I felt a tug on my pants leg and jumped about thirty feet in the air. Tim O'Leary was under the table, peering up from between the crepe paper ruffles and bunting.

"*Shh,*" he said, finger to his lips, before disappearing back under the table.

"Elias, could you watch Tim for me?" Mrs. O'Leary asked. "I can't seem to find Shohei."

I looked over at my dad, who was ready to go ballistic after spotting Jason Takeshita's project, "The Mystical Powers of the Pyramid." I nodded, then followed Tim.

We ended up in the Atrium Garden, where Tim fetched pennies from the Fountain of the Grand Army of the Republic, until it was time to go.

Honoria

After I splashed my face off in the locker room, I serenely, majestically even, exited, and promptly bumped into Shohei who, as usual, wasn't looking where he was going. My silver medal clanked to the tile floor.

"Sorry," Shohei said, stooping to pick it up. As he handed

it back to me, Shohei gave it a glance, then said, "Congratu-lations," but it was more like a question than a declaration of principle. Then, when I said nothing, he added, "You won the silver."

I almost laughed. Last Olympics, I had gone off exten-sively on how awful it was that the broadcasters had called the silver medalists "losers."

"Why," I asked, "does everyone treat me like I wouldn't deeply appreciate the honor of winning second place at the Peshtigo School science fair?"

He gave a quirky grin, then observed more seriously, "You actually *like* the science fair."

"You think?" I asked.

Shohei ignored that. He gestured toward the gym. "You like this whole pile of . . ." His voice trailed off. He held up my medal. "Goliath Reed likes *this*. He comes up with projects he knows he can win at. You do projects because you actually want to learn stuff. You're, like, a *scientist.*"

"Thanks," I said, after a moment, "for trying to make me feel better. But Goliath Reed actually won at the science, too." I showed Shohei my score sheet. The only thing I'd had any serious points taken off for was my fake plants, which supposedly did not constitute a sufficiently controlled envi-ronment.

"Plants!" Shohei said. "Ugh."

At my raised eyebrow, he explained. About Tim and the *ikebana* and the results he'd faked by copying Christoph.

"I'll bet Eli was pretty —"

"He did that clenched-jaw, teeth-grinding thing," Shohei said, nodding.

"That's serious," I agreed.

"It'll be okay," Shohei replied. "Look, I have to go . . . I've got to find Tim." Then he ran off.

It was one of the longest one-on-one conversations I'd ever had with him, I realized. And then I started to wonder why.

Chapter 20

Bad News

Elias

My science fair participation certificate came with an itemized score sheet. Scores were given for Appearance and Presentation, Methodology, Lucidity of Explanation, and, of course, Scientific Validity. I scored a zero on Methodology and a zero on Scientific Validity.

Because I didn't think it was fair, I went to speak to Mr. Eden, to get some explanation and maybe even score one or two extra points. It was worth a try.

I'd never been in his office before. It had a window overlooking the Atrium Garden and portraits of Bach and Handel. It was kept way too warm and even more humid than the Atrium Garden itself, probably for Mr. Eden's creepy collection of carnivorous plants. The place smelled vaguely like a swamp and the Christmas tree–shaped car air freshener hanging in the window.

My glasses fogged instantly.

"What do you want, Mr. Brandenburg?" Mr. Eden asked me, his image blurry. He was hunched over one of his plants. "No, don't tell me. I suppose you're here about your science fair assessment."

"You gave Shohei a B," I said.

He'd gotten low points for Appearance and Presentation, but high points for Scientific Validity. Ha.

"Mr. O'Leary burned his eyebrows with a Bunsen burner last year," Mr. Eden said, wiping his fingers on his handkerchief.

"So?" I asked, my glasses finally clearing.

"Mr. O'Leary's effort was a good one, by the standard by which he ought to be judged. Yours was not."

I couldn't believe that Mr. Eden was judging us on different standards for the same project. "Do you know how much I worked on that project?" I asked.

"Irrelevant," Mr. Eden said, now caressing a Venus flytrap. Its jaws snapped shut. "You copied the work of your brother Johann Christoph, and even with that advantage, you weren't able to get it right. Mr. O'Leary *did* obtain the correct results."

"How do you know Christoph got it right?" I said.

"Child," Mr. Eden said, standing upright, and looking

down at me. "You are the sixth member of your family I've taught. You have the potential to be more than the runt of the litter. And yet, your project was clearly a failure. It took less effort, showed far less imagination than anything even Johann Jakob ever presented."

"What?" I asked.

"The football player," he said, as if the phrase offended him.

"I know who —"

"Look!" Mr. Eden exclaimed, pointing out his window into the Atrium Garden. "Since Christoph's experiment, we have treated the Garden to the most exquisite and transcendant music mankind has to offer. Johann Sebastian Bach. Antonio Scarlatti. George Frederic Handel. Antonio Vivaldi. Johann Pachelbel. Georg Philip Telemann. The flora have never been so lush or vibrant. *Quod erat demonstrandum.*"

"But, that's so completely wrong," I said. Something else could be causing it. If it was even true. "How do you know the plants aren't growing better because they changed the recipe for Miracle-Gro?"

"Mr. Brandenburg. You. May. Leave," Mr. Eden said.

I stood, but asked, "Why did you approve the project in the first place?"

Mr. Eden glared. "The science fair is not about original research. That is why Mr. Reed wins despite his rather banal conceptualizations. The science fair, indeed, science, is about *method.* About how you go about your experiments. Your project could have been an excellent, independent research project. Instead, it was a cheap and tawdry imitation of your brother's." He took a sip of coffee. "Go. Now."

I went.

Chapter 21

Troubles

Shohei

So I was lying on my *tatami* bed in the dark, tossing a soccer ball at the ceiling. Elias wasn't talking to me and I wasn't ready to talk to him yet, anyway.

Worse, almost, dinner with the Eichbaums and the bonsai class were just a few days away. I mean, I was supposed to be celebrating, or whatever, my Japanese heritage. But my parents had never let *me* decide what that meant.

When they'd remodeled my room, I'd wanted to put up a couple of samurai swords. My mom had said "no" because they were "not going to glorify a sordid military tradition." They'd vetoed my Godzilla film festival idea. Too violent, they'd said. *Anime* was out for the same reason, and, no, I have no idea why they let Tim do the ninja thing.

The Chicago Auto Show? Cars are a major cause of global warming, they'd said.

The Consumer Electronics Show? Video games are bad for the eyes, and besides, the show was too far away. Yeah, it was in Vegas, so I'll give them that one.

But since Japanese is my heritage, I figured I should at least get to choose what parts to get in touch with. It's not like we're living in Japan where you don't have a choice other than to become one with it. Besides, I *was* learning the language. I mean, my parents don't speak anything other than English! Dad's totally Irish American, and Mom probably is, too, but also maybe part Lithuanian and Polish, depending on who her real grandfather is. They're only a couple generations off the boat, but they've never had any interest in learning more about where they came from.

I caught the soccer ball and sat up. My parents and I were going to have a little talk.

But first, I needed to do some shopping.

Elias

The more I thought about it, the madder I got. I'd spent as much time on my project as Honoria or Goliath Reed. And my science was right. I didn't expect a medal, but a C was ridiculous. Especially since Shohei had gotten a B. It wasn't fair. I had to do something to get Mr. Eden to listen. To show him he was wrong.

And it had to be something spectacular.

Still, I probably wouldn't have thought of it if Number Two Son, Johann Ambrosius, Chess King and Spymaster, hadn't taught me how to open a locked door with a piece of coat hanger.

It's quite simple:

1. Cut about a six- or eight-inch piece of coat hanger (the wire kind) with any suitable wire-cutting tool. I prefer needle-nose pliers with a cutting edge.
2. About an inch and a half from one end, use the pliers to bend the coat hanger to about ninety degrees.
3. Make a matching bend at the other end but in the opposite direction. This allows you to easily manipulate the resulting implement.
4. Insert your newly-created tool between the door and the frame, where the doorknob latch is.
5. Push the doorknob latch in.
6. Open the door.

Note 1: Don't try this at home.

Note 2: The above method does not work with dead bolts.

Note 3: The control room for the Atrium Garden does not have a dead bolt.

Chapter 22

Ninja Acts

Elias

After soccer practice Friday, I hid in the locker room. I'd told my dad I was going over to Shohei's. I figured I could take the El home, or maybe a cab.

When I was sure everyone else had left, I sneaked out. I stayed close to the hall lockers, trying to hide in the shadows. I figured I could avoid the janitors, but I wasn't taking any chances.

At night, the Peshtigo School isn't completely dark, since the glow of the city's sodium-vapor lights shines through the Atrium skylight and classroom windows. But there's this weird quiet — not a silence, since you can hear the traffic outside on Grand Avenue, Illinois Street, and Lake Shore

Drive. And, of course, in the Atrium Garden itself, the sounds of the glorious baroque. It's kind of neat and a little creepy.

I climbed the stairs to the fourth floor. Outside the control room, I shined a penlight at the door and inserted my coat hanger fragment between the door and the frame. Seconds later, I was inside. It took only a minute to find the CD player Mr. Eden used for the plants. Out went *Ode for St. Cecilia's Day,* and in went the CD I had bought at lunch.

It was a song I'd liked when I was little but that Dad forbade in the house on first hearing.

It was poetic.

It was catchy.

It was "Puff, The Magic Dragon."

Shohei

I'd just finished putting on my fake tattoos when the doorbell rang. I waited a couple minutes for the knock on my bedroom door.

"Shohei," my dad said through the locked door, "the Eichbaums are here."

"Be there in a second, Dad," I called.

I touched up my face paint and waited for a couple more

minutes. I did a final check. My hair was spiky and chemical neon green. I had shamrocks on my cheeks. I was wearing a Notre Dame Fightin' Irish TOUCHDOWN JESUS T-shirt and green soccer shorts, and I was holding a big, green foam rubber WE'RE #1 finger-glove thing.

I was ready.

I cracked open the door to make sure no one was in sight. My parents, Tim, and the Eichbaums would all be in the living room. My parents loved to show off the view of the lake.

I sneaked down the hall. I paused a moment, listening for voices, to make sure everyone was there. It was the point of no return. I could get into mega-trouble. Probably would.

I jumped into the room.

"Top o' the evening to you!" I shouted, waving the WE'RE #1 glove.

They sat there, stunned. Mr. and Mrs. Eichbaum were next to each other on the sofa, Megan and Mallory were side-by-side on the love seat. Dad was standing at the bar, and Mom was sitting in one of the armchairs.

"Mom, Dad," I said into the silence. "I think you have to get in touch with your Irish heritage. I want to be as supportive as possible. You need to buy lots of tam-o'-shanters, shamrocks, and potatoes. You should also remodel Tim's room like a mud hut, or stone cottage, or whatever."

Still not a word from my parents. Mallory looked at me like I was a little kid, beneath her notice. Megan and the Eichbaums, though, were definitely trying not to laugh.

Then I started to sing "It's a Long Way to Tipperary" as loud as I could.

That's when I was tackled from behind.

"Gotcha!" Tim yelled.

I pitched forward, with him on top of me. My legs got tangled in his cape and he tried to snatch the glove. So I held him down and started to pummel him with it.

"Mom!" he yelled. "Shohei's hitting me!"

Somehow, he managed to squirm free. He took off down the hall. I stood, pausing long enough to look at the Eichbaums. "Hi, I'm Shohei," I said. "*Sláinte.*" Then I raced after Tim.

Honoria

Eli and I were in the hall, just outside the leaded glass French doors leading to the wrought-iron entryway to the Atrium Garden. It was Monday morning before classes. There wasn't anyone too close, but we were keeping our voices down.

"You did *what?*" I asked Eli, not because I hadn't heard him, but because I couldn't believe I'd heard him correctly.

He'd just told me he had sneaked into the Garden Friday night to change Mr. Eden's CDs.

I was horrified. Mr. Eden was a little harsh on Eli sometimes, but this was way out of line. "What if they find out? They'll expel you."

"But it'll prove to Mr. Eden that the new music won't affect the plants," Eli replied.

I held my history book to my chest. "How?"

"He'll see that the plants don't die, or get dry rot, or wilt, from the music," Eli replied, a little smugly.

"Okay," I said, "but what do you think Mr. Eden played in the garden *before* he switched to chamber music?"

Eli went a little pale. "I don't know," he said.

I shook my head. "You better hope they don't notice or, if they do, they don't catch you."

"Oh, they'll notice," Eli said, with a grimace.

"A word of legal advice," I said. "Say nothing, admit nothing, deny nothing."

"Hmph," he replied.

Chapter 23

Meeting the Vice Principal

Elias

They came for me during seventh-period algebra.

Ms. Chang was discussing the history of the Traveling Salesman Problem when Mr. Eden and Vice Principal Harrell opened the door. Mr. Harrell's official title was Vice Principal of Student Affairs, which meant he was in charge of discipline, student conduct, and behavior modification. Mr. Harrell walked over to Ms. Chang and whispered something. They both looked at me. Then she said, "Mr. Brandenburg, you're excused from class."

I decided to take Honoria's advice. Say nothing, admit nothing, deny nothing.

I stood, gathered my books, hoisted my backpack onto my shoulder and marched, eyes forward, up the aisle and out the door. I walked between Mr. Eden and Vice Principal Harrell, through the science wing, past the cafeteria, around the Atrium Garden.

No one spoke.

We arrived in Vice Principal Harrell's corner office. It faces east and has a lake view. The first thing I noticed, other than the uncomfortable-looking Frank Lloyd Wright rip-off furniture, was the TV and VCR sitting on a cart.

Vice Principal Harrell sat behind his desk, folding his hands. He wore little round wire glasses and a navy suit with a smiley-face tie. A cabinet along one wall held trophies. Behind him loomed a print of the Mile High skyscraper that never got built. Next to it was a poster that read, IT TAKES A VILLAGE TO RAISE A CHILD.

"Johann," Vice Principal Harrell said, "you may know that, here at the Peshtigo School, we try to resolve our problems as a community."

I said nothing. Clearly, something bad was about to happen.

Vice Principal Harrell held up a videocassette and moved to insert it into the machine. "I would like to show you something."

On screen, a grainy, black-and-white image of me appeared, entering the control room and fiddling with the CD player. The time stamp showed that it was 5:30 P.M., well after school hours.

Incriminating evidence.

This was very, very bad.

"Nice," I said. "Do you have cameras anywhere else I should know about?" I swear, I was momentarily possessed.

"Now, Johann," Vice Principal Harrell said, sitting back at his desk, hands folded once more, "your anger is not what we call productive." He shuffled some papers. "We would like to help you become a more fulfilled and self-actualized member of the Peshtigo School family —"

"Mr. Brandenburg," Mr. Eden cut in, sitting on a desk corner, "we are referring this matter to the Student Court. You are to be charged with malicious hooliganism and vandalism."

"Vandalism?" I repeated. "What vandalism? *Nothing* happened to the plants!"

Vandalism was, I don't know, spray-painting gang graffiti on the school walls, or taking a sledgehammer to the audio-visual storage room, or any other good, old-fashioned, random, wanton destruction and violence.

Vice Principal Harrell shook his head sadly. "I am afraid that Mr. Eden," and he gestured at Mr. Eden, "has insisted that you stand trial for your actions."

Mr. Eden spoke again. "By changing the CDs, you removed the flora from the beneficial effects of the baroque music environment, thereby inhibiting their potential growth and, hence, causing them damage. The flora is school property. Damaging school property constitutes vandalism. Punishment for vandalism can range from detention to expulsion." He smirked. "The trial will commence Monday."

I gripped the wood arms of my chair. There was no way that he could've seen any kind of damage to the plants. They were healthy before "Puff." They were healthy after "Puff."

"Of course," Vice Principal Harrell said quickly, "you are presumed innocent until found guilty by a jury of your peers." He steepled his fingers. "That's the beauty of the system. As I'm sure you're aware, the Peshtigo School Student Court has been featured as a model in *Newsweek* magazine . . ."

I left Vice Principal Harrell's office feeling numb. I walked this time without an escort. I guess they weren't afraid I was such a delinquent that I would act out my rage against the Peshtigo School family with further acts of vandalism and malicious hooliganism.

They were, they said, going to call Dad, and they did not need me there.

The question was, would Dad be more upset that I would, possibly, be expelled, or that my "Puff, The Magic Dragon" demonstration had been conducted without a control?

The expelled part, probably. But only by a hair.

What would happen then? Dad would, maybe, disown me, never speak to me again, unless I became his only hope for grandchildren. Not likely, since I had a sister and four older brothers. Mom, though, would make sure I stayed in school. Not public school, even though both of them had gone to public schools and I hear they're really improving.

Catholic school? We weren't Catholic. We weren't even particularly Protestant, except in a go-to-church-on-Christmas-and-Easter sort of way.

That left the Lab School at the University of Chicago. I began to panic. I'd heard about what goes on there. They're not all touchy-feely like Mr. Eden. They make you work.

All the time.

And, it's just down the street from my dad's office. I'd have to commute with him. He could take advantage of that tuition break he was always talking about.

I was doomed.

Chapter 24

The Justice System

Honoria

At the Peshtigo School, the wheels of justice turn very swiftly. By the time I got to the ninth period student court meeting, Eli's case, *Students of the Peshtigo School v. Brandenburg,* had already been docketed, and a trial date had been set for next week.

"This one's mine," Goliath Reed told me, as he handed me a copy of the charges. He held up four fingers and then left for football practice.

Andrea Shaw brushed past me to sit at the opposite end of the conference table, as far away from me as possible. We hadn't spoken a word since her warning me about her man. That reminded me, I hadn't heard anything about Eli's e-mail "from" Shohei in a while. I briefly wondered if he'd send another now that they were mad at each other. Or at least, Eli was mad at Shohei. Shohei just felt wretched and pathetic. Which he was.

Maybe, I thought, I should just talk to Shohei myself.

Josh Patel cleared his throat, and I looked up. Everyone was staring at me, waiting to begin.

"Then it's mine, too," I said, full of false confidence. Even though I'd lost four cases in a row to Goliath, I still had the best record. Certainly Andrea Shaw wasn't equipped to take on her boyfriend, Josh still had to deal with the root beer incident, and Wendy McCormick and Angela Palsgraf needed a lot more practice.

Besides, Eli was my friend.

Elias

When I got home from soccer practice that day, Dad was playing his cello and Beastmaster VII was hiding in the living room underneath the Flemish double harpsichord. I considered barricading myself in my room, but figured it was time to face the music. I climbed the stairs to my funeral and knocked on the doorframe. I stood in the doorway while Dad finished up the *bourrée* from the C Major Suite No. 3, BWV 1009.

He pointed at me. "Sit."

I sat. Deep armchair with wings that kept me trapped.

He said, "I understand you have a date in court."

"It's not my fault," I said, gripping tight to the armrests.

"Did you break into the music room?" he asked.

"Yes."

"Did you switch the music in the Garden?"

"Yes."

"Did you have permission to do either?"

"No."

"Then it was your fault," he said. He leaned back into his chair. "It may interest you to know that I spoke with your mother." I sat upright, my mouth dry, and wondered inanely what time it was in Australia.

"She sends her love," Dad continued, "and told me to give you these." He gestured at a pair of volumes sitting on his desk blotter in front of him.

"What are they?" I asked.

"The libretto from *Rigoletto* and an Italian-English dictionary," Dad replied. "Your mother wants it translated into English by the time she gets back." Then he handed me a fountain pen and a pad of stationery. "Longhand. And be prepared to discuss it."

I took the pen and pad. "Is that all?" I asked quietly.

"Not quite," Dad answered. "You are hereby grounded. For ten thousand years. Go to your room and do not come out."

♪

Shohei

By the middle of the week, I was starting to get worried. My parents still hadn't had The Talk about my ethno-pride display for the Eichbaums, though they'd done a great job during the dinner and ever since of pretending everything was normal. As for Elias, he still wasn't speaking to me. I'd tried to call him, but he'd just hung up.

So maybe it wasn't such a great idea to copy Christoph's old data. But how was I supposed to know that Elias would get it wrong — sorry, "fail to confirm" — too? The whole reason Elias did the project was because it was supposed to be easy. And following his lead should've been even more of a no-brainer.

When the phone rang just after dinner that night, I grabbed it, thinking it might be Elias. Honoria's voice said "hi," and I handed Tim the phone. Ignoring his chants of "Shohei's got a girlfriend," I ran to my room, where I picked up the line and yelled at Tim to get off it.

"What's up?" I asked Honoria.

"I'm defending Eli in Student Court on charges of vandalism and malicious hooliganism, and I need you to testify about your project," she said.

"What did he do?" I asked.

Honoria filled me in on Elias's ninja act in the Garden. Wow. It was pretty extreme, for Elias. Kind of neat, though. Sort of wish I'd thought of it. I would have loved to have seen Mr. Eden's face when he came in on "Puff."

"So, anyway," Honoria said, "I need you to testify that you falsified your results. Would you be willing?"

I didn't say anything for a moment. Elias was going way overboard being mad at me, and his break-in wasn't real smart and that wasn't my fault. But he was still my friend. "If it'll help," I said.

"It could count against you as academic dishonesty," Honoria warned. "You could get detention or be expelled. I'd have to look it up."

"Wait," I said, thinking it through. "Are you saying that Elias and I got the right results and Christoph and Mr. Eden have it wrong?"

"That's what I'll argue. That music doesn't help plants grow. Not baroque music. Not 'Puff.' Nothing. It may even be the truth," Honoria replied. "But, like I said, admitting you cheated could get you expelled. Probably should."

I thought a moment. If Honoria could pull this off, she

could probably fix it so I wouldn't get expelled either. Besides, I kind of liked the idea that Mr. Eden was wrong. And Elias might un-freak a little. "It's okay," I said. "I'll do it."

"Good," Honoria said. "Oh, and would you like to go to *Riverdance* this weekend? My father got tickets as a thank-you from a client."

"The Irish dance thing?" I laughed. "I'd love to."

Elias

My being grounded for ten millennia did not, apparently, include conferring with counsel. Saturday afternoon, my father delivered me to Honoria's to go over litigation strategy.

She was seated on the opposite side of her mother's library table from me. She was wearing a dress that made her look sort of curvy. She had some black smeary stuff under her eyelashes, and her lips were shiny. "What's wrong with you?" I asked.

She frowned. "What do you mean?"

"Why do you look like that? We're just working on my case. It's not like it's school picture day or anything." Not that Honoria had ever dolled up for a school picture.

"Shohei and I are going out to *Riverdance* later," she explained. "It's practically our first date. I look stupid, don't I? I feel stupid."

Since when did either of them date anyone, let alone each other? Shohei wasn't supposed to like her. I was going to have to kill him. Again. Slowly.

"You don't look stupid," I said quietly, trying not to show anything. "Sort of early, though, isn't it?"

"I wanted to be prepared for the possibility that I wouldn't have time to change later," she replied. "Now, to get back to your case, I talked with my father about your vandalism and malicious hooliganism and —"

"So what is 'malicious hooliganism'?" I asked Honoria, opening her copy of *The Peshtigo School Rules of Public Safety* and pretending my life wasn't falling apart.

A real date.

"Any nonspecific activity the administration doesn't like," she replied. "It's very flexible."

"Why not breaking and entering?" I asked, leafing through the Rules. I wondered if Shohei would try to kiss her.

"It's unlikely that they can charge you with that," Honoria said. "The regulation defined it as 'entering school premises after hours without permission.' Inasmuch as you were already on school premises when you changed the CDs, they probably can't get you that way."

"You know," I said, bringing up the jerk again despite myself, "I can't believe what a lousy job Shohei did on his project."

"You know," Honoria told me, toying with a mechanical pencil, "it's pretty rotten of you to bad-mouth him when he's coming over early to go over his testimony that he pretty much faked his experiment. It's courageous, don't you think?" She looked at me. Calmly.

"He's going to testify?" I exclaimed. "I don't believe it."

"Now," Honoria went on, "in order to prove that you're guilty of vandalism, they have to show that you caused damage to school property, in this case the plants in the Garden. If there was no damage, there's no vandalism."

I stood up to pace on the Oriental rug.

"For that," she continued, "we have your experimental results."

"Two things," I said slowly, my eyes catching a jar of ladybugs on a shelf, "One: my experiment doesn't prove that music has no effect on plant growth. And two: my experiment doesn't prove that 'Puff, The Magic Dragon' has no effect on plant growth." All I had shown was that I had not confirmed Christoph's results. We didn't really know anything.

"I know that you can't prove a negative," Honoria said. "But we don't have to. *They* have to prove that music *does* affect plant growth. They have to prove classical music helps the Garden grow and that 'Puff' stunts it. All *we* have to do is introduce a 'reasonable doubt' that the music doesn't matter either way. Plus, for show, there's also the fact that the Atrium Garden didn't wither and wilt, or whatever you were going for, when you changed the CDs."

Her doorbell chimed, and Honoria jumped up. "That's Shohei," she said. "Are you going to behave?"

"Me?" I asked. "He's the one who —"

"Behave," Honoria said, pointing at me.

I nodded, telling myself I would, for her benefit, not his.

Shohei walked in with her a few minutes later. He was wearing a charcoal, double-breasted suit, a red paisley tie, and his hair was green. Neon green.

For a moment we just stood there, staring at each other.

Thanks to Shohei, my science project had been a disaster. I had to translate an entire opera about a guy who accidentally causes the death of his own daughter while trying to take someone else's life. I was grounded for ten thousand years. I was getting a D+ in science. And Honoria still wanted to go out with *him*.

Still not a word.

Then Honoria said, "Right then. It's a start. I'm going to get some Cokes." She left, leaving Shohei and me alone.

"Look," he said, "I'm sor —"

"Can we just get to work?" I asked.

"Look," Shohei said, again, sitting down, "I don't have to do this —"

"You didn't have to blow off my project, either!" I said. "I was doing you a favor. You begged. 'Ple-e-ease, help me, help me, help me.' Remember?"

That shut him up a minute. But just a minute. "Just because you're Mr. Eden, Junior," he replied, "doesn't give you the right to tell me —"

"I am not," I said, "Mr. Eden, Junior."

"Oh, please," Shohei leaned forward on the table in front of me. "You even sound like him. 'You must do the experiment with proper scientific blah, blah, blah, blah.'"

"Listen, you overdressed leprechaun," I said, standing to face him, "I'm not the one who burned his eyebrows off. I'm not the one who cheated on his science project. And I'm not the one who can't see that Honoria's madly in love with them. Him. You."

And then I heard what I'd just said. It couldn't have been me that said that, though. It must have been someone else. I was watching.

"What?" Shohei exclaimed.

"Eli!" Honoria said at nearly the same time. She was standing in the doorway holding three cans of Coke. "You promised!"

She stared at me, then glanced at Shohei, turned around, and fled.

Shohei watched her leave for a moment, then glared at me and followed her.

So much for the case.

My life.

And our all being at least friends.

Chapter 25

∫he Likes Me

Shohei

Honoria liked me? I had no idea. I mean, she was a great friend and everything, but *liked* me? She's cute and all, but — at the risk of being fed to the piranhas — she's not really my type.

I followed Honoria upstairs, then stood in the doorway to her room a moment, not sure what to say.

"Out!" she yelled, pointing. She was sitting on her bed in the middle of a pile of books, clutching what I found out later was a stuffed porcupine.

"I'm sorry," I said, turning to leave. "I wouldn't have written the e-mails for Elias if I'd known —"

"Wait," she interrupted. "*You* wrote them for *Eli?*"

"Um," I said. "Yeah?"

"Your invitation to *Riverdance* is hereby revoked," she declared. Then she threw an atlas at me.

I ran.

Chapter 26

Emergency E-mail

Elias

E-mail to Number One Son, Johann Christoph:

```
Christoph—
I'm getting a D from Eden because I
didn't get your results.
Help!
Call.
Write.
E-mail.
Send a telegram.
Or a carrier pigeon.
SOMETHING.
—Elias
```

Chapter 27

Pretrial Procedure

Honoria

I spent the rest of the night in my attic bedroom thinking about baking Shohei and Eli into blood pies, like in *Titus Andronicus,* and feeding the results to Spot and Fluffy. Then I thought of not bothering with the pies at all and just sticking them into the microwave, and pricking one with a fork to see which one, if either, would explode. Then I just thought.

Eli liked me. It was as if somebody had just told me that the earth was flat, and all of a sudden I realized that I believed it. But I still couldn't believe he'd ratted out my feelings to Shohei. Of course, if he liked me himself, it probably wasn't a big thrill listening to me babble on about Shohei all the time. I let out a long breath.

Eli liked me.

When I woke up the next morning, I decided that disemboweling my two so-called best friends probably wouldn't be productive over the long term. It would do nothing to alter the fact that I felt like a complete idiot. How could I have not known Eli liked me and Shohei didn't care? Or at least, that Shohei didn't care the way I wanted him to care.

The fact that I still had to work on Eli's case just seemed cruel. But there was no way Mrs. Talmadge would let me withdraw at such a late date. So I was stuck with it.

Elias

Monday morning. Eight-thirty. My trial was scheduled for that day after school. I hadn't talked to Honoria since Saturday. She'd temporarily disconnected the telephones. At least, that's what the voice mail greeting said.

I hadn't tried to call Shohei.

I didn't know if Shohei and Honoria had still gone to see *Riverdance* after I'd left. I didn't know if they were going out, period. What if *I'd* brought them together?

That morning, I went to the library to see the Student Court sponsor, judge, and extremely reasonable person. "I'd like another lawyer," I said.

"Why?" Mrs. Talmadge asked.

I hesitated. "Personal differences."

"Tough," Mrs. Talmadge replied.

"I beg your pardon?"

We were in her office, the room where they used to keep the mainframe. It was the only part of the library that didn't smell like books. I was sitting in one of the two leather Chicago White Sox chairs in front of Mrs. Talmadge's gray metal desk, which matched her hair. Resting on the desk in front of her was a statue of St. Ivo, patron saint of lawyers. The caption read A LAWYER, BUT NOT A THIEF.

"It is too late in the process to change lawyers," Mrs. Talmadge said.

"But —"

"I don't want to hear it," she cut in. "I strongly recommend that you speak with Ms. Grob today before your trial starts. However, if you don't, here is all the administrative information you will need." She handed me a thick manila folder. "You're scheduled to meet with Ms. Grob during ninth-period study hall."

I glanced inside the folder. *The Peshtigo School Rules of Trial Procedure.* All one hundred and thirty-six of them. I needed Honoria.

"Sit down, shut up, and stay out of my way," Honoria said.

I decided not to ask how her evening with Shohei had gone.

We met in the R.J. Morris Courtroom just before trial. Benches for the witnesses and spectators were separated by an aisle. The lawyers sit up front at the two big tables. The judge's dais is front and center, and the witness stand is this gated thing with a chair. The jury — usually students a year or so older than the accused — perches to the left, in front of the stained-glass windows. All thanks to some generous alum with too much money.

Honoria was sitting at the defendant's table in front of the bar, gnawing on her pen.

I was still standing, wondering if Honoria and Shohei had declared their mutual love. "Look," I began, not sure what to say next.

Honoria took the chewed pen out of her mouth. "I might allow you to grovel later. Right now, I'm your lawyer. Sit."

"Okay," I said, and sat. I was quiet for about a minute. Then another one. "What's all this?" I asked, opening the folder that Mrs. Talmadge had given me.

"This is not shutting up," Honoria informed me.

"But why are these witnesses . . . ?" I showed her the sheet.

"I've seen it," she told me, busily scribbling my best hope for salvation.

"I can understand why the prosecution is calling Mr. Eden as a witness," I said, taking the chair beside her.

"Shohei, too. But what does Freddie have to do with any of this?"

Honoria paused briefly to glare at me.

I leaned back in my chair.

"Why aren't they going after Freddie?" I asked. "Her animal rights kooks and their paint caused real damage." Now *that* had been vandalism.

"Plea bargain," Honoria replied. "Freddie and the Murchettes got off by agreeing to testify against you."

I glanced at Honoria's list of legal vocabulary and at the yellow pad, her bug-leg handwriting scattered all over, huge chunks scratched out.

"It's my opening statement, all right?" Honoria said, her voice nervous.

I was gonna fry.

Chapter 28

Opening ∫tatements

Honoria

Because the prosecution gets first stab at opening state-
ments, Goliath Reed was up first, and, as usual, he stood and
dramatically buttoned his suit jacket.

"Ladies and gentlemen," he began, "Johann Elias Brandenburg broke into —"

"Objection!" I exclaimed. Goliath Reed was always trying
to take advantage and inflame the jury. It was so annoying.

"Sustained," Mrs. Talmadge said, looking at Goliath Reed
over the rims of her silver half-glasses. "The jury will disregard the last remark."

"What was that?" Eli whispered.

"We've stipulated that you changed the CDs," I whispered

back, without taking my eyes off Goliath Reed. "So your breaking-and-entering performance isn't relevant. He can't bring it into this hearing. Ethically, anyway."

"How'd you manage that?" Eli whispered.

"Don't ask," I replied without turning my head.

". . . And the only bit of supposed science to support the idea that plants aren't harmed by his music," Goliath continued, "is Mr. Brandenburg's own science project. The weight of evidence proves otherwise." He sat.

The jury had followed his every move. This early in the trial, they were still paying attention.

Next, it was my turn. "Ladies and gentlemen of the jury," I began, "this trial is about the fact that someone has dared to question the common, accepted, and flat-out *wrong* view of the natural order." I walked to the jury box, looking the jurors, one by one, in the eye. "About heresy, in fact. In the good, old-fashioned, medieval, cursed-with-eternal-damnation, burning-witches-at-the-stake type of way. Heresy of the same kind that got Galileo Galilei threatened with excommunication for asserting that the earth revolves around the sun.

"You see," I continued, stopping in front of the jury, "Mr. Eden and the Attorney General here believe that playing music can harm a plant. My client, Johann Elias Brandenburg, has conducted experiments that show this belief to be as absurd as the notions that the earth is flat, or that the moon is made of cheese. His experiments have shown that music does not, in fact, affect plant growth."

A couple of the jurors actually sat up.

I glanced at my notes. "Mr. Brandenburg acted upon his scientific conclusions by introducing," I went on, "a little variety into the musical selections to which the Atrium Garden is usually subjected." Which was the most flattering and least stupid way I could describe what Eli had done. "Because of this, he is accused of vandalism."

I walked toward Goliath Reed, who was scribbling on his own legal pad. "The prosecution," I said, "has to prove, beyond a reasonable doubt, that Mr. Brandenburg's actions caused *some destruction* — that's the definition of vandalism — *some destruction* in the Atrium Garden. Only if the prosecution proves that beyond a reasonable doubt can you convict my client. Now," I concluded, "Peter, Paul and Mary's song 'Puff, The Magic Dragon' may be a lot of things, but the central question is: Do you really think that singing hippies can affect plant growth?"

Chapter 29

Mr. Eden to the ∫tand

Honoria

Goliath Reed called Mr. Eden to the stand first.

"Mr. Eden," he began, "about ten years ago, Mr. Johann Elias Brandenburg's older brother, Mr. Johann Christoph Brandenburg, conducted a science project that led you to begin playing music" — he checked his notes — "of the baroque period in the Atrium Garden, did he not?"

"That is correct," Mr. Eden replied, folding his hands. "Christoph was one of my most outstanding students."

Goliath paused, smiling at the jury, to make sure they got the point. "The experiment showed," he continued, "that playing such music to plants will improve their growth, but that other types of music, or no music at all, can harm them."

"Objection!" I stood. "Your Honor, that is exactly what is at issue here."

"Good," Eli whispered to me.

"Shut up," I muttered back. The jury should see him paying attention, not looking gossipy. I had too much to worry about without having to baby-sit.

Mrs. Talmadge toyed with her gavel. "Sustained. The jury will disregard that last statement."

"I'll rephrase, Your Honor," Goliath said, picking an imaginary piece of lint off his lapel. "It is your expert opinion that the experiment showed that baroque music has a positive effect on plant growth."

"Yes," Mr. Eden said.

Goliath pretended to make a mark on his legal pad. "Why did you believe those results?"

"Because," Mr. Eden answered in his chem lab lecture voice, "Christoph Brandenburg followed rigorous and conscientious procedures while conducting the experiment."

"I see," Goliath said, walking in front of the jury. He turned back to Mr. Eden. "Have you ever known the defendant, Elias Brandenburg, to use improper laboratory procedures?"

"On occasion," Mr. Eden replied, "he has attempted to conduct chemistry experiments without the benefit of goggles."

"It was sugar water," Eli protested, voice low.

"*Shh,*" I told him. "Try to look innocent and trustworthy."

With his back to the jury, Goliath smiled at Eli. Eli smiled back.

I kicked Eli under the table. "Ignore Goliath," I whispered. "He just wants you to react for the jury."

"Since Christoph Brandenburg's experiment," Goliath said to Mr. Eden, "you've been playing classical music to the plants?"

"I have, and the Atrium Garden has never been as luxuriant."

Goliath Reed walked to his table and lifted an envelope. He pulled a handful of Polaroids out. "I'd like to introduce these photos as Exhibits A through M. Pictures of the Atrium Garden."

I glanced through them, then nodded. "No objection."

Goliath gave them to the bailiff, who handed them to the jurors. They looked through them as though they'd never been to the Garden.

"Mr. Eden," Goliath said, "please describe these pictures for the jury."

"This group of photographs shows the Atrium Garden in all its splendor," Mr. Eden pronounced. "As you can see, the chenille plants have never been so lush, the avocados so exuberant, or the orchids so sublime."

"No further questions," Goliath announced, returning to his table. "Your turn," he mouthed at me.

Even though I'm always a little nervous when I begin cross-examination, I was worse that day, because it was Mr. Eden on the stand. I arranged my papers a moment to calm myself and wondered briefly if that was why Goliath always buttoned his suit jacket at the beginning of his statement.

"Mr. Eden," I said, standing for the cross-examination, "you've indicated that Elias Brandenburg's experiment is not valid because he once forgot to wear a pair of goggles in chemistry lab. In the entire history of science, has anyone ever established a scientific connection between music and protective eyewear?"

"The point is —" Mr. Eden began.

"Please answer the question," I replied. It was the first time I'd ever interrupted him.

"Not to my knowledge," Mr. Eden said, scowling.

"Mr. Eden, you've testified that Christoph Brandenburg was both 'rigorous and conscientious' in the conduct of his experiment," I said, reading off my notepad. "Did you ever once observe him being 'rigorous and conscientious' while conducting a music and plant growth experiment?"

"No, I did not."

"How could you know his procedures were 'rigorous and conscientious'?" The question was a gamble. On cross-examination, you're supposed to stick with yes-no questions

146

so the witnesses can't go off on their own. I was trying to set him up.

"Because I watched Johann Christoph in my chem lab. I know that Johann Christoph knew how to, and would have, conducted such an experiment in a rigorous and conscientious manner."

Leading him on, I said, "So you believe Johann Christoph's experimental results because you have faith in Johann Christoph, the experimenter?"

Mr. Eden paused. "You could put it that way."

"I see," I said, zeroing in. "So, what do you believe Johann Christoph Brandenburg is doing with his brilliant scientific aptitude today?" Another gamble.

"I am sure," Mr. Eden said, "that he is engaged in the advancement of analytical human knowledge."

"So he wouldn't, for example," I continued, "decide to go corporate?"

Mr. Eden locked his arms behind his head. "Hardly," he said. A moment later, he sat up straight, his arms flopping down. "Wait, are you saying that —"

"Yes," I informed him. "Johann Christoph Brandenburg quit his postdoc at Cambridge University to start up an Internet computer game company." I paused for effect. "Perhaps you are making some false assumptions."

I heard some laughter from the jury box. I was very careful not to turn to look at them. I did have a pang of worry, though, that I'd just made it onto Mr. Eden's "most persecuted" list.

"Getting back to the business at hand," I continued, shoving aside that concern for the moment, "it is customary, is it not, for follow-up experiments to be conducted, to try to confirm or reproduce supposed groundbreaking results?"

"Generally, yes," Mr. Eden said, shifting in his seat.

"Has anyone done so?"

Mr. Eden pointed at Eli. "The accused," he said, "attempted to do so."

"Attempted?"

"Well, he clearly failed," Mr. Eden said.

"Why 'clearly'?" I already knew the answer.

"He did not achieve the same results as Christoph, even using the same experimental apparatus." Mr. Eden leaned back in the witness chair. "Despite the influence of classical music, Elias's plants did not grow."

"Oh, one more thing, Mr. Eden," I said, turning back to him. "Those pictures, were they taken today?"

"Yes," he replied.

"The pictures you're using to show the health of the Atrium Garden were taken *after* the so-called vandalism?"

"Well, you see —" Mr. Eden began.

"No further questions," I interrupted, dismissing him.

148

Chapter 30

∫hohei to the ∫tand

Shohei

"Mr. O'Leary," Goliath Reed began, "you ran the same experiment as Mr. Brandenburg, didn't you?"

"Yes," I replied. Honoria had told me that since Goliath Reed had called me as witness for the prosecution, he'd want to talk to me first to go over testimony. He never had, although the fact that I missed our appointment — twice — might have had something to do with it.

The questioning continued, with Goliath looking down every now and then at his legal pad. Yes, I had the same apparatus. Yes, the procedures were outlined to be the same as mine. I looked over at the jury.

"Mr. O'Leary," Goliath asked me next, "did your experiment show that playing music to plants can affect their growth?"

This was it. "Yes" would help Goliath's case. "No" could wreck it.

"No," I replied, "it didn't."

Goliath dropped the pad. "What?"

"Yeah," I said, running a hand through my green hair. "My plants all kind of died. Well, they were killed when my kid brother Tim *ikebana*-ized them. It was too late to get more. I figured I knew what was supposed to happen, and so I copied my results."

I looked over at Mr. Eden. He was giving me one of his "you-are-scum" looks. I smiled at him, even though it probably meant I was going to get that D+ Elias seemed so worried about.

"I," Goliath paused, "have no further questions."

Honoria passed on questions, too.

"As the next witness," Goliath Reed said, "I call Ms. Frederika Murchison-Kowalski."

"Your Honor, I object to this witness," Honoria cut in. "Her testimony is of no possible relevance."

"Your Honor," Goliath said, "it goes to whether the defendant has a history of carelessness in the conduct of science."

Mrs. Talmadge toyed with her gavel. "I'll allow it," she said.

Honoria sat.

"Ms. Murchison —" Goliath began.

"Killer!" Freddie screamed and stood in the witness stand, pointing at Elias.

All the jurors woke up. Goliath Reed stood there, jaw hanging open. Mrs. Talmadge gripped her gavel, like she couldn't believe what she'd heard.

"Killer!" Freddie screamed again. "I know what you did to those mice! I was in the lunchroom!"

"Order!" Mrs. Talmadge banged her gavel. "Ms. Murchison-Kowalski, if I hear —"

That's when the chanting started. Someone had let in the Murchettes. "Mice are nice! Fry that guy! Mice are nice! Fry that guy!"

Mrs. Talmadge cleared the courtroom.

Chapter 31

Verdicts

Elias

It took the jury only twenty minutes to decide my fate.

The twelve filed back into the courtroom, and then Honoria and I stood to face them. About half of the jurors met my gaze. That was supposed to be a good sign. The rest looked elsewhere. That wasn't. The foreman, Jason Takeshita, handed Mrs. Talmadge a slip of paper. She read it, then nodded, handing it back.

"On the charge of malicious hooliganism," Jason said, reading off the slip, "we find the defendant not guilty."

I wanted to hug Honoria. If she'd looked over at me, I might have.

Jason continued, "On the charge of vandalism, we find the defendant guilty."

"What!" I exclaimed.

Honoria shushed me.

Mrs. Talmadge thanked the jury and dismissed them.

I was packing papers into my backpack and getting ready to go, too, when Honoria whispered, "Stop that. She's going to sentence you now. Look contrite."

I dropped my stuff and looked at Mrs. Talmadge.

"Mr. Brandenburg," Mrs. Talmadge began, "for vandalism, *The Peshtigo School Rules of Public Safety* give me a great deal of equitable discretion in deciding your punishment, from none at all to expulsion."

I tried harder to look contrite.

"I'm not going to expel you," Mrs. Talmadge continued. "Instead, I'm going to give you a choice."

I glanced at Honoria, who shrugged.

"Your first option is a two-week suspension," Mrs. Talmadge said. She paused, maybe to let that sink in.

A two-week suspension was bad, even horrible, but it was better than expulsion. I could at least argue to Dad that I was partially vindicated.

"But I hope you'll take the second option." Mrs. Talmadge closed her notepad. "Mr. Brandenburg," she said, looking at me, "we seem to be here today because of your refusal to accept Mr. Eden's reasoned judgment that your experiment was flawed and your results mistaken. Therefore, rather than suspension, I give you the option of publicly apologizing to Mr. Eden for damage to the Atrium Garden and admitting that, in light of what we have seen presented in this courtroom, your project was flawed. In other words, to use the analogy that Ms. Grob has been attempting: apologize and recant.

"You have until tomorrow to decide," Mrs. Talmadge concluded, punctuating the sentence with a bang of her gavel.

"Galileo's choice," Honoria murmured.

I nodded. It would be easy to recant. Say I'd made a mistake and go on with things and accept the D+. But my results were legitimate. My experiment had shown that the music had no effect on the plants. No way I was going to confess to something that wasn't true.

"Galileo recanted," Honoria told me after a minute.

"I know," I said. "But he was right. The earth does revolve around the sun."

"Sometimes, being right doesn't matter," Honoria said.

I took the El home from school that night. It was a bit of a hike to the station, but I felt like the walk, despite the wet chill. I finally got on the train and had to stand, holding on to one of those stainless steel poles, jammed in between a woman in a black trenchcoat and a guy in a stained Chicago Bears windbreaker.

My cell phone rang. It was Number One Son, Johann Christoph. Considering he was calling from England, the connection was pretty good. "So," I said slowly, "don't you read your e-mail?"

"Not often," he replied. "Mom told me to call. She said you broke into Eden's Sanctum."

"Yeah," I replied, turning up the volume on the handset as another train went by. "Are you ever going to explain to me exactly how music can affect plant growth?"

"Well," he began, "sound waves are just vibrating air molecules, so if there was enough power —"

"Itty-bitty speakers," I said.

"How's this? The music psychically affects the plants in, you know, the same way it soothes the savage, um, breast."

"Psychically?" I repeated.

There was a pause. I had to dodge people as they got on and off the train.

Then, I knew. The reason we got the different results. Christoph had pulled a Shohei. Fraud. Pure and simple. I couldn't believe it. Mr. Paragon of Science himself was a cheat. I couldn't decide whether to laugh or cry. Maybe both.

"Why did you fake your results?" My voice remained steady.

There was a noise on the other end, sort of a cross between a choking sound and a chuckle. "It was a couple of things," he answered, carefully. "Sort of a practical joke and sort of a bet I'd made with my chemistry lab partner. Whether we could convince Eden to change the stuff he used to play in the Atrium Garden. I never thought I'd win."

I don't know what I'd been expecting, but this was really lame. My reason for changing the music wasn't great, either, but at least there was some *science* behind it.

"You were like, what, a year old or something at the time? You used to spit up and leak a lot, and your head was lumpy," Christoph continued. "How was I supposed to know that you'd try to do the same experiment for the same teacher?"

I was definitely older than one, but I didn't bother correcting Esteemed Older Brother. I was more worried that there would be no correcting Mr. Eden. There was no way Mr. Eden would believe the truth. He had been playing baroque to the vegetables for more than a decade. Because of Christoph's practical joke. It was almost . . . operatic.

"Listen," I said, "because of your 'practical joke,' Honoria and Shohei aren't speaking to me, I'm probably going to be suspended, I'm getting a D+, and I'm the only one here who's gotten the science right. But does anyone give me any credit for that? No! Mom's making me translate *Rigoletto* and Dad's grounded me for ten thousand years!"

The lady in the trenchcoat wedged in next to me gave me a weird look.

156

"Tell you what," Christoph said. "I'll talk to Dad and Eden, if you want. But for what it's worth, Dad told me that you did a great job on the project. He even said it was 'nontrivial.'"

"Yeah," I said, "right."

I looked out the window of the train as we pulled up to the Belmont stop. I got off to make the connection to the Ravenswood El.

"What was it?" I asked finally, when the train had cleared. "What did Mr. Eden used to play?"

"Nineteen-fifties classic rock. You know, Buddy Holly. Elvis. Chuck Berry."

"You're kidding," I replied.

"No," Christoph said. "Really. He owns half of Eisenberg's Rock & Roll Café, too, did you know?"

"No, I didn't," I said. "Okay, talk to Dad. But I don't think it would do any good to talk to Mr. Eden. He'll just think you're trying to bail me out. You did too good a job of brain-washing him."

I hung up as the Ravenswood train arrived.

Chapter 32

Decisions

Honoria

After I had put all my books and notes and the rest of Eli's case file back into my locker, I went outside to wait for my mother on the main steps of the school. Across the street, I saw Shohei eating curly cheese fries in a window booth at Eisenberg's.

He never had noticed me. Not with the mice or even the invitation to *Riverdance*. He'd even helped Eli — or tried to — with that really awful e-mail campaign. I'd had enough waiting and wondering and throwing myself at him.

Ignoring the drizzle, I crossed at the light and pulled the door open. As the warmth hit me, "It's My Party" wailed.

I slid into the booth across from Shohei. A plate of half-eaten fries sat on the table.

"Hi," I said.

"Oh, hi," Shohei replied, sitting up.

"You have ketchup on your nose," I said.

He wiped it off. "Um —"

"I just wanted to let you know," I interrupted, "that I don't want to go out with you anymore."

"Does that mean you're breaking up with me?" he asked, with a crooked grin, but he did look, I think, a little disappointed.

"You had your chance," I said.

He nodded, then gestured at the plate. "French fry?"

Shohei

I knew it was coming. The Talk. I'd expected it earlier, but Dad had been working late. So we played the "we'll pretend it didn't happen until we're ready to talk" game. Very polite and very weird and very my family.

When we finally sat down at the kitchen table, I was ready. Before my parents could say anything, I asked, "So could you tone it down with the whole turning Japanese thing?"

"We just don't want you to lose out on something you need," Mom said.

What did that mean? I tried to break it down. My parents

usually weren't insane people. This time, though, they were nuts. Sure, it was a big deal they were into my emotional well-being and all, but I didn't *need* sushi, *tatami,* bonsai, or *ikebana.* What was next? Origami? Karate? *Harakiri?* "News flash," I said, "all the teriyaki in the world isn't going to —"

"It is part of you," Mom interrupted.

"Yeah," I said. "But lots of things are part of me. Japan. America. Chicago. Ireland . . . sort of. Soccer. My friends. Mathilda. Being adopted. I just want to be the one who gets to choose what the parts are and what they mean."

I took off my Cubs hat, showing the green hair. "You guys have picked how much Irish you want to be. Why can't I?"

With that, Tim ran up and started hitting me on the back of the head with the WE'RE #1 foam finger. "Then there's this weird kid we found on the street." I turned around and grabbed the foam thing from Tim and began hitting him with it.

"Shohei's hitting me!" Tim yelled.

My mom laughed as Dad grabbed the finger and began to pummel both of us with it.

When things settled down a bit, Dad said, "Okay, you've made your point. We won't *make* you sample Japanese culture if you don't want to."

"But we will keep introducing you to aspects of it," Mom put in.

"Fine," I said. But they were definitely up to something. It had been kind of too easy.

"Does this mean you don't want to spend a month in Japan next summer?" Dad asked. "There's a program one of my clients told me about —"

"Really? Wow. Sure!" I said, immediately. I'd never been to a foreign country before. Other than Canada, but that didn't really count. Who wouldn't want to go?

"And you could try out your Japanese," Dad continued.

"Wait a minute," I said. "Was this the plan all along, or something you guys just made up?"

"Does it matter?" Mom asked, after she and Dad exchanged one of their looks.

"I guess not," I said, but I had this feeling I'd been royally set up. Parents. I was going to have to watch them.

Elias

Back in my room at Castle Brandenburg, I asked Beastmaster VII, "What do you think I should do?"

He yawned. Big. Dramatic. Dog breath.

"Not helpful," I told him, leaning back on my bed.

Recant or be suspended.

It was odd. After all that had happened, we still didn't quite know the truth. Even if my process had been a hundred percent correct, there was no confirmation that baroque music doesn't help plants. Not that you could prove a negative. But another run-through would have been helpful. Thank you, Shohei.

But, to be fair, Shohei's cheating was all that I had a right to be mad at him about. He wasn't the one who'd broken into the school to change the music. It wasn't his fault Honoria was in love with him. He *had* 'fessed up to his own scientific fraud. Publicly. Even after I'd yelled at him. And I wasn't really fair to him. It wasn't his fault I got all obsessive about the fair and grades and Mr. Eden.

Maybe Shohei was right. Maybe I'd been too much like Mr. Eden. Too self-centered. Maybe I needed to work on that. Probably.

Now, if I only knew what to do about Honoria.

Chapter 33

Apologies

Elias

I finally called Shohei. "Thanks for testifying," I said, settling in at my computer. "I'm sorry I came down on you that way."

"That's okay," Shohei said. "It's who you are. It's why we know and love you."

Despite myself, I laughed.

"Did my testimony help?" Shohei asked.

"Probably not," I replied.

"I *am* sorry I blew off the experiment."

"But aren't they going to suspend you or something," I asked, it just occurring to me, "for academic dishonesty?"

"Nah," Shohei said. "Honoria says even though it can count toward your grade, the Science Fair's officially an extracurricular activity, so the Academic Code doesn't apply. But they might ban me from next year's fair."

"Well, that's good. Both," I said, checking my e-mail and not finding any replies from Honoria to my eighth e-mail of abject groveling. "Honoria's pretty mad at me."

"Oh, yeah."

"So are you going to go out with her?" I asked, hoping I sounded casual, in an academic, not-interested way. I didn't think I had a chance anymore, but it would still be hard seeing them together. I clicked "New Mail" again. No new messages.

"She dumped me," Shohei said.

"Oh?" I asked. Calmly. Waiting for more.

"Yeah," Shohei replied, "she said it took me too long to notice her. That we'd always be just friends. I still think it's you she likes."

I tried to sound merely curious. "Because?"

"I think she liked the idea of my having Mathilda, in that weird animal kind of way she has. But when you talk to her, it's always 'Me and Eli, this' or 'Me and Eli, that.'"

Well, that sounded promising. More than promising. Maybe something could work out between Honoria and me after all. I surfed over to the JustBugs web site, remembering the mice she'd given Shohei. Maybe a gift of some kind.

"By the way," Shohei said, "my folks finally got the message about Japanese America. No more Land of the Rising Sun. But I'm going to Japan this summer for a whole month."

"Sounds great," I replied, a bit distracted, but glad he'd finally gotten that worked out.

Bugs were too impersonal, I decided. Even leeches.

"Yeah, but they're talking about getting season tickets for Notre Dame football," he said. "You know, Irish."

"Soccer football or football football?" I asked.

"Football football," he said. "I think they're joking, but just in case, what are you doing on Saturdays next fall?"

♪

Honoria

After dinner, I was upstairs in my bedroom reading my favorite biography of Marie Curie, nestled under an afghan my grandma had crocheted, on the cushioned bench next to the front window. I turned the page and heard music from outside.

I looked out. Eli was standing on our front porch playing his electronic keyboard. Beethoven's *Pathetique* sonata. I clicked the remote to turn off my Ella Fitzgerald CD. After a moment, he finished and looked up hopefully.

I opened the window. "I thought you were grounded," I called down.

"I escaped to apologize," Eli said.

"I got your e-mails," I told him. "Pretty sad."

"You don't have to talk to me if you don't want. I'll just leave this between the doors." Eli held up a thick red folder. He opened the screen door and set it down.

I said nothing while he unplugged the electronic piano and then made a call on his cell phone. For a ride, probably. He stood there a moment, looking across our lawn toward the street. He shivered. He looked pathetic. And he *was* trying to apologize.

I marked my page and went downstairs. Sometimes I'm just too nice or, maybe, just not mean enough.

When I opened the door, the red file folder fell at my feet. I opened it as Eli entered. "Your sister's planaria experiment!" I exclaimed. Raw data and everything. It had been the *best* high school project last year. The best one ever, in fact.

"In living color," Eli replied. "Laser copied, anyway. Daily logs and all. Everything except the actual flatworms."

"You're still in trouble," I said, "but thank you." We needed to talk. At the very least, he was my best friend. At most, well, I was still not thrilled with him. But Eli had potential. "Why didn't you feel you could tell me how you felt about me?" I asked, as we headed in to the library.

"I would have," he replied, "but the way you were mooning over Shohei —"

"I was not," I said, sinking into one of the brown leather chairs, "*mooning* over Shohei."

He glanced down at me. "I know. I'm sorry," he repeated.

"I was planning," I told him, "to stay mad at you for at least a month, angry for another week after that, and then mildly irritated for the next three days."

He swallowed hard, looking a bit wary. "But?" he asked.

"But I guess I could get it over with now," I said. He was trying. "Just don't ever tell anyone one of my secrets again. Ever. Or I will feed you to the fishes."

Chapter 34

Plans

Elias

It felt great to have everything fixed up with Honoria and Shohei, or at least better. Sort of. But I still had a problem. After I sneaked back in, I lay awake in bed, trying to decide which Student Court sentence to accept. Even though Dad was leaving it up to me, I knew he wouldn't be happy with a suspension. But I also thought he'd felt that my experimental results were correct. And so did I.

It was my choice.

At two o'clock in the morning, I decided I didn't like either option. The only thing to do was to change the rules. I was going to need some help to pull it off, though. I speed-dialed Honoria and conferenced in Shohei.

"Hi guys," I began. "What are you doing first thing in the morning?"

Chapter 35

∫entencing

Elias

The next morning, before classes began, Honoria and I ambushed Mr. Eden at the Memorial Fountain of the Grand Army of the Republic. He was there, as usual, with a spray bottle and pruning shears in hand, weeding or delousing or whatever he does to the plants.

"What are you doing here?" Mr. Eden demanded.

"My client has a proposition for you," Honoria said. She held up a jar. "This jar holds one hundred and twelve healthy and pregnant specimens of *Melanoplus devastator*, commonly known as the devastating grasshopper. *M. devastator* is known to devour a wide selection of grasses, shrubs, and trees." She looked around the Garden meaningfully. "They're very hungry."

"Dear Lord, give me that!" Mr. Eden exclaimed, his mouth twitching as he lunged at Honoria.

"Stay back," she said, jumping away and turning the lid counterclockwise once. "This isn't the only jar. Shohei! Tim!"

Shohei emerged from beneath the equestrian statue of James Clerk Maxwell. From the opposite end of the Garden, Tim jumped from behind the side-by-side busts of Gottfried Leibniz and Isaac Newton. Each O'Leary clutched a jar of *M. devastator.*

Tim spread his black cape like bat wings.

"I see," Mr. Eden said. "Pray continue."

I held my breath. This was it.

"My client is willing to re-create his experiment with your cooperation," Honoria said, "to promote the progress of the horticultural arts. He is not willing to recant. Mr. Brandenburg is similarly unwilling to accept a suspension.

"However, if you are willing to make a statement today, Mrs. Talmadge will probably withdraw those parts of Mr. Brandenburg's sentence."

Mr. Eden pointed the spray bottle at Honoria. "And if I am not?"

Another counterclockwise turn. "'For they covered the face of the whole earth, so that the land was darkened; and they did eat every herb of the land, and all the fruit of the trees . . . and there remained not any green thing in the trees,

170

or in the herbs of the field, throughout the land of Egypt.' Exodus ten, verses four through six. King James Version."

"I see," said Mr. Eden. "You realize, of course, that I could have you all expelled."

"Perhaps," Honoria continued, hand still clutching the lid. "But that wouldn't help your Garden or advance the cause of science."

Mr. Eden was silent a moment, probably trying to decide whether he would prove himself a fanatic or . . . less of a fanatic.

♪

Honoria

Sentencing was ninth period in the Student Courtroom. This time, there was no jury and only a handful of spectators. Just Eli and me, Goliath Reed and Judge Ruth Talmadge, presiding over the sentencing of one Johann Elias Brandenburg.

"Where is he?" Eli asked, playing with a fountain pen.

Mr. Eden wasn't there. It was almost time for Eli to panic. Me? I was nervous, too. Goliath Reed was slouching, relaxed in his chair, looking hugely pleased with himself.

Shohei and Tim were our insurance, still holding onto jars of grasshoppers in the Atrium Garden. They were so much alike it was funny.

"Mr. Brandenburg," Mrs. Talmadge said, looking at him,

"have you reached a decision? Will you accept the suspension or apologize to Mr. Eden?"

"Your Honor," Eli said, standing, "I'll —"

"Excuse me!" Mr. Eden dashed into the room and up to the bar. "Your Honor, I'd like to make a statement."

Mrs. Talmadge smacked her gavel into her hand, then gestured with it. "If Mr. Brandenburg has no objection."

"No objection, Your Honor," I said.

This was it.

"Your Honor," Mr. Eden began, "since the entire matter depends on the extent of Mr. Brandenburg's scientific acumen, I propose, rather than the punishments that you have outlined, that he be required to repeat his experiment. Under my supervision, of course."

Mrs. Talmadge looked at Mr. Eden, then at Eli and me, then back to Mr. Eden. Then she leaned back in her chair and stared at the ceiling for a moment.

Finally she spoke, focusing intently on Mr. Eden. "Something is going on here." I suppressed a grin as Mr. Eden actually *squirmed,* but he didn't let on what the something was. Finally, Mrs. Talmadge banged the gavel. "Very well," she said. "Mr. Brandenburg, you are remanded into Mr. Eden's custody."

I almost cheered as Eli let out a breath. But before we could celebrate, Mr. Eden walked up to us. "This is for you," he said, handing Eli a file folder. "I've delineated a procedure for conducting the experiment. Read it carefully and be prepared to discuss it in my office at seven A.M. tomorrow." Before Mr. Eden walked off, he whispered something to Eli that I didn't hear. Eli looked puzzled, but before I could ask him, Goliath Reed walked up.

"I'll see you at the next court meeting," Goliath said, then walked out.

That was it. No acknowledgment of my brilliant victory. Nothing.

I didn't care. I didn't have to do the Penguin dance to be a winner.

Chapter 36

Back in the Garden

Shohei

Elias, Honoria, Tim, and I met up later in the Garden. Very faintly, over the splash of the fountain, Mr. Eden's baroque music was playing again.

"You won your case," Eli told Honoria. "Thanks."

"Well," she said, smiling, "I doubt that the American Bar Association would've approved of our tactics."

Tim bowed and presented Honoria with her jar.

I grabbed a leaf off an avocado tree. "So could these guys really destroy this place?"

"They could," Honoria replied, putting the jar into her backpack, "but only if there were about a million of them, and only if these were, in fact, *M. devastator.*"

"What!" I exclaimed.

She shrugged. "These guys are just *M. confusus* — the pasture grasshopper. They like ragweed. They wouldn't eat the stuff in here." She frowned. "Probably. I think."

"That's what he meant," Elias said, looking a little pale.

"What?" Honoria asked.

"Just before he left," Elias told her, "he said to me, 'I *know* everything.' He knows you were bluffing about the grasshoppers."

"No way," I said before Honoria could. But I was glad I wasn't going to be the one redoing the experiment with Mr. Eden. We glanced at each other uneasily.

A moment later, I spotted something near Tim's foot. Tim dived under the bench and grabbed it.

"Mouse!" he said, standing up and opening his palm.

"Must be your third mouse," Eli said to me, looking at the white rodent. "Or should I say, Mathilda's third mouse?"

Honoria peered close. "That's not her."

Then I saw another one dart across the path. And another.

We all looked around, scanning the undergrowth. We looked at each other.

"You know," Honoria said, pulling an encyclopedia entry from memory, "the average litter for *Mus musculus* is twelve.

The average gestation period is twenty days. The life expectancy is about two years, they can reproduce at five weeks, and they're herbivores."

I didn't bother with the math. Mr. Eden would have to bring in some cats.

Soon.

Author's Note

As Honoria noted, Elias is not the first scientist to have been tried or criticized for publishing results that challenged long-held but experimentally untested beliefs.

Galileo Galilei (1564–1642; usually referred to, for some reason, by his first name) was an Italian physicist, mathematician, and astronomer who had a big mouth and a vicious pen. He's particularly noted for experiments in mechanics and dynamics that refuted certain long-held but experimentally untested scientific beliefs, which had gone down to Renaissance Europe by way of the Greek philosopher Aristotle. (The story of Galileo dropping lead weights off the Leaning Tower of Pisa to see when they would hit the ground, unfortunately, appears to be fictional.)

Galileo was a proponent of the view that the sun, not the earth, is at the center of the solar system. Because of his publications to this effect and defiance of various church edicts, Galileo found himself condemned by the Holy Office of the Roman Catholic Church (a branch of the Inquisition) as "vehemently suspect of heresy" but — like Elias — was given the option of recanting. Unlike Elias, Galileo recanted, perhaps because in his case the penalty for heresy was excommunication and, possibly, burning at the stake. In the end, Galileo abjured his errors, and signed a document "cursing and detesting" them. Galileo was subsequently condemned to house arrest for the rest of his life, a fate Elias avoided. I think. The Roman Catholic Church, under Pope John Paul II, has since admitted its own errors regarding Galileo.

Dr. Brandenburg, Elias's father, has a bizarre fascination with the life and works of the German composer Johann Sebastian Bach (1685–1750), possibly because his name is the same as one of Bach's most famous groups of compositions — the Brandenburg Concertos, named for the Margrave of Brandenburg, one of the Electors of the Holy Roman Empire. There are, perhaps coincidentally, six Brandenburg Concertos.

Because of his Bach obsession, Dr. Brandenburg gave his children Bach family names. Johann Sebastian Bach's second wife was Anna Magdalena. He had a cousin named Johann Elias. His father was Johann Ambrosius and his uncles included a Johann Christoph and a Johann Jacob. Johann Ambrosius and Johann Christoph had a cousin Johann Michael and another cousin Johann Christoph.

To those poised to enroll at the Peshtigo School, in hopes of taking Mr. Eden's chemistry class, don't. The school doesn't exist. But if it did, it would be located in Chicago on Peshtigo, between Illinois and Grand, near Lake Shore Drive and Navy Pier. Old time Chicagoans will recognize this as the site of the old Kraft Building.

To answer the question: Can you teach a piranha to eat a banana? Surprisingly, there's no need to. Piranhas are by nature omnivores. Some species of piranha, in fact, almost exclusively eat fruits and vegetables.

However, the answer to Honoria's true experiment, whether you can teach a piranha that he'd rather eat a banana than flesh, remains a mystery, though experts I consulted doubt it. And since piranhas are illegal in Texas, I am unable to pursue the matter on my own.

As to Elias and Shohei's experiment, trying to determine whether playing music to plants affects their growth, the scientific results are inconclusive.

This novel could not have been written without the support, help, and/or technical assistance of the following:

She Who Is My Wife, Cynthia, for everything

Anne Bustard, for most excellent midwifery

Kathi Appelt, for hostessing a certain
Brazos Valley and Austin SCBWI writing conference

Ginger Knowlton, my agent, and Amy Hsu, my editor,
who were undoubtedly brainy kids themselves

In my writing group:
Jerry Wermund, Betty Davis, Meredith Davis,
Jimmy Hendricks, Frances Hill

the experts at the Lincoln Park Conservatory,
Chicago, Illinois; the Wisconsin Fast Plants Project
at the University of Wisconsin, Madison; and the
John G. Shedd Aquarium, Chicago, Illinois

Teachers of Science, Math, and English:
Mr. Lewis, Mrs. Biddulph, and Mr. Mims;

and

my parents, Esther and Albert.

Greg Leitich Smith has a few things in common with Elias, Shohei, and Honoria. Like them, he grew up in Chicago and survived the science magnet school experience. Afterward, he went on to complete degrees in electrical engineering from the University of Illinois at Urbana-Champaign and the University of Texas at Austin, and earned a University of Michigan degree in law.

In addition, Greg drew on his own Japanese-German American background in crafting Elias's and Shohei's families — especially Shohei's. Like Shohei, Greg is adopted, and they both have one brother, although Shohei's is younger and Greg's is older. Greg now lives with his wife, author Cynthia Leitich Smith, and their four cats in Austin, Texas.

As to his life experience with all things ninja and spymaster . . . he refuses to comment, on the grounds that he might incriminate himself.

www.gregleitichsmith.com